To & Fro

Leah Hager Cohen

Bellevue Literary Press
New York

An Invitation

Herein: two beginnings with nary an end
Unless, perhaps, an invisible friend

Could count as a destination?
Pray drop expectation

Of where things are bound—
Simply start here or flip it around.

Fro

Turn it and turn it, for all is therein.

—Pirkei Avot 5:22

Onion

Annamae Galinsky was serious to a fault. She'd been that way as long as anyone could remember, even in the crib. She was not glum. She didn't lack a sense of humor. She was just serious. About most things. Joy included.

Everyone who knew her agreed on this without disparaging her for it, or if disparaging her, doing so fondly. "Lighten up, Annamae," her older brother liked to say. This never had the intended effect, but, rather, its opposite: It made her feel heavy. The weight of being reminded she was alone.

"But you're not alone," her brother would point out.

"Danny," their mother would say. "Respect her feelings."

"What!"

"She means lonely."

She didn't, though. She meant alone.

Would it always be this way?

As a little girl, Annamae had been susceptible to earaches and spent many painful hours convalescing in her mother's bed, cradling half a warm onion against the infected ear. Her mother, a scientist, said there was no data to support the use of onion poultices. Nevertheless, she would always slice an onion, heat it in the microwave, wrap it in one of her late husband's wool socks, and deliver it to Annamae in bed.

They lived in a narrow three-story building in the part of the city where the streets bunched and ran crooked. Annamae's mother's room was on the second floor, just off the kitchen. The children's rooms were on the third floor, along with the bathroom. Their part of the first floor was nothing, just the skinny vestibule at the bottom of the stairs, cluttered with a coatrack, mitten bench, boot tray, umbrella stand, recycling bin, scooters, knapsacks, and library books that needed returning.

Annamae's mother's room was large and peaceful. Whenever one of the kids was sick, it was the infirmary. A person could lie there in all the spaciousness of the queen bed, which smelled faintly of apricot hand cream, and hear whoever was in the kitchen, talking or just puttering. A person could call, even feebly, for things she wanted and know she would be heard. Through the window, which faced the street, a person could see into the lit windows of the office building across the way.

"There's not a shred of evidence it does anything," her mother would say as Annamae, her face flushed with fever, held the half onion like a seashell to her ear.

Yet it did seem to help.

"Can you hear the ocean?" Danny would tease.

"No. Shh."

"What are you listening to, then?"

"Messages."

"What do they say?"

"They're not for you, Danny."

The other thing that seemed to help were picture books, the kind with elaborate illustrations in which a person could lose herself. Annamae's mother had a particular, unhurried way of reading to her children. She would linger on each page, sometimes musing out loud ("Do you see that kitten peeking out of the girl's pocket?" "Which of those bicycles would you choose?" "I wonder where that road leads, after it goes over the hill. . . ."), other times silently touring the image with a fingertip.

Sometimes she was busy and Annamae just lay in an exhausted sort of tension and looked out the window.

On winter afternoons, when dusk came early, the building across the street turned into a giant honeycomb. Each window a cell. Some glistened brightly, as if with honey. Others were dark, as if sealed with wax. In the honey-filled cells, figures the size of her pinkie finger moved about. Sometimes they walked from one cell, the light snuffing out behind them, only to emerge in another. She couldn't make out their faces from this distance. Just their triangle skirts, rectangle pants, semicircle hair. The simplified shapes of paper dolls. On certain feverish afternoons they became her living dolls and she would tell them stories about themselves, narrating what she witnessed as it unfolded. Sometimes she would make a game of trying to anticipate their actions, to say what they'd do before it happened.

"Once upon a time there was a lady who had a cup of coffee," Annamae would whisper from her pillow. "She walked over to the window and poured it—it was really water—on her plant.

"Once upon a time a guy stood up from his desk and stretched. Then he looked at his phone, but there weren't any messages, so he put it back in his pocket."

Whenever their actions mirrored her words, it gave her the funniest feeling. A moment's exhilaration, as if she'd won the game—followed by a cold pit in her stomach. To think she really was in charge of inventing their world.

Science

"She's not a real scientist," said Danny. He was fifteen months older.

"Yes she is," said Annamae.

They took the dispute to their mother, who was sitting at the wooden picnic table with built-in benches that was their kitchen table. Surrounding her was a fort made of her laptop, a pile of manila folders, a yellow legal pad, pencils, journals, and books with lots of different colored stickies marking the pages. She was wearing her "readers."

"You are a scientist. Right?" asked Annamae.

"Riiiight . . ." Their mother did not take her eyes from the screen. The word stretched into two or three syllables, faint as pencil on wet paper.

"But you're not a *scientist* scientist," said Danny. "Right?"

"Riiight . . ." Still looking at the screen. She was doing that thing she did of stroking where her mustache would be if she had a mustache.

"But!" said Annamae. "You can't just agree with both of us."

Now their mother turned to them. She took off the readers and placed the tip of one clear green plastic earpiece in the corner of her mouth. "That is also right. Said the rabbi. Ha ha."

They both knew the rabbi joke, and Annamae's mouth opened a little bit in delight when she realized they had accidentally perfectly set up the punch line.

But Danny said, "Mom, don't fake laugh."

"That wasn't a fake laugh. A fake laugh would be this"—she fake laughed—"whereas I said, 'Ha ha.' Which is more an indication of awareness that I'm being silly."

This. This was how their mother was.

Linguistics

The kind of scientist she was was a linguist. That meant she didn't wear a white coat or pour things out of test tubes. Linguistics was the study of language. Some people really loved having long debates about whether things were art or science or a combination of both, and whether things were hard science or soft science and which was better, but their mother said what she really loved was studying the relationship between language and psychology.

"Like feelings," said Danny.

"More like how the brain processes language," said their mother.

The kind of linguist she was was a developmental psycholinguist. That meant she studied language acquisition during the critical or sensitive or optimal period when neuroplasticity is most operative. She and her colleagues used something called the mel-frequency cepstrum to quantify timbre in the speech of mothers interacting with their babies because what she really particularly studied was motherese.

"What's that?" Annamae, who had drifted over to the fridge to play with the alphabet magnets when all the science-sounding words, with their sharp metallic tang, started coming out of her mother's mouth, perked up at the word *motherese*. "Is it a real thing?"

"Motherese is what linguists call the special way mothers—or really any caregivers—speak to their babies."

Annamae used her finger and thumb to pull out her bottom lip. An upside-down mirror version of her mother's imaginary mustache thing. "Tell the rabbi joke," she said.

The Rabbi Joke

> Moishe and Sammy are having a dispute. They can't come to an agreement, so they go to the rabbi. Moishe lays out his side of the argument. The rabbi listens, nods, says, "You're right." Sammy says, "Wait, you haven't heard my side." So he lays out his side of the argument and the rabbi listens, strokes his beard, and says, "You're right, too." The rabbi's wife, who's been there the whole time, says to her husband, "What do you mean? They can't both be right." The rabbi looks at her for a long moment. "*Nu,*" he says, "You also are right."

"Why doesn't the rabbi's wife have a name?" is what Annamae wanted to know the first time she heard this joke.

"Oh," said her mother. "I guess she doesn't really need one for the sake of the joke."

"Neither do Moishe and Sammy. You could just say two guys."

"That's true," said her mother. "But it wouldn't be as funny."

The Rabbi

The rabbi was short. Four foot eleven. She had springy reddish curls and gold-rimmed glasses and a perfect mole tucked below one eye. She always wore a brightly colored crocheted yarmulke bobby-pinned to her hair. Other than that, you wouldn't know she was a rabbi.

Their mother had met Rav Harriett when their father was dying. This was such a long time ago, neither Annamae nor Danny would have remembered it even if they'd been there, which they hadn't. But they knew the story as if they had.

Their mother had stepped out of the hospital room because her phone rang and she didn't want to disturb their father, who was resting. The person on the phone was *her* mother, Nana. At that moment, when their mother was on the phone in the hospital corridor outside their father's room, talking with Nana, Nana was at their home, taking care of Annamae and Danny, who were both still babies. So in a way Annamae and Danny were in the story, too. But they were not the important part, because this story was about how their mother met Rav Harriett, who just at that moment was clacking down the corridor in her low high heels to visit their father's room to see if he or their mother wanted to speak with a chaplain.

Finding their mother standing outside the room, Rav Harriett smiled at her in a way that was clearly an invitation to pause her phone conversation, yet without being pushy. So their mother had said to Nana, "Can you hang on just a minute, Mom?" and returned a flickering attempt at a smile. "Yes?"

Rav Harriett, pointing first to the laminated hospital badge she wore around her neck, and then to the yarmulke that her curls might have hidden if she hadn't been so short, introduced herself and explained that she had come by to see if "Mr. Galinsky or you" would like any spiritual support.

"But," she said, with a nod toward the phone in their mother's hand, "perhaps you're already receiving spiritual support?" It was clear she understood their mother was on the phone with *her* mother, and from the way she said it, their mother felt that Rav Harriett had marked something true and good. And it *was* true and good. Nana really was that person in their mother's life.

So their mother had said, "Oh. Yes. Thank you. I am. Thank you," probably still looking tired and worried but now also smiling back in a way that was less flickering and more real, and said, *Thank you for seeing what is real.*

Rav Harriett had looked toward the door to their father's room, which was closed, although you could see him through a pane of glass, and before their mother could say that he was resting, which was her instinct—to leap in and protect him from a visit from a stranger—Rav Harriett had looked back at her and said, "I see. You're in good hands."

And their mother hadn't known whether Rav Harriett meant because she was on the phone with Nana, or if she meant something else that she'd been able to tell just from looking through the pane of glass at their father lying there, or if she was talking about God. But after Rav Harriett left, and their mother had gone back to talking with Nana on the phone, she felt different. It wasn't a feeling like hopeful or comforted. It was more of a physical feeling, right in the center of her body. As if she'd swallowed some salty golden broth.

She didn't see Rav Harriett again until after their father had died, when she contacted the director of the hospital chaplaincy to ask the name of that female rabbi with the reddish curls and gold-rimmed glasses.

"What were we doing?" is what Annamae wanted to know the first time she heard this story.

"When?" said her mother.

"When Nana was on the phone with you and she was taking care of us."

"Oh. I don't know," said their mother. "Probably sleeping."

Mail

Annamae decided to write the rabbi a letter.

Dere Rav Harryet,

Mom toled us the story abowt you it is a longe time sins you vizited lassed time we had pie.

Love,
Annamae

"What's that supposed to say?" asked Danny, looking over her shoulder. She was sitting on a bench at the wooden picnic table. He had come past her on his way to make chocolate milk.

Annamae read it out loud to him.

"She's not going to have any idea that's what it says."

"Yes," countered Annamae.

"Want me to help you spell it right?"

"Excuse me, I have to go to the post office now." With dignity, Annamae folded the paper in half, sealed it with a piece of Scotch tape, walked across the room, and mailed it between two folds of the accordion radiator.

"Oh," said Danny.

"Now I'm going to write the Fairy Man," said Annamae. "You can help me spell this one if you like."

Fairy Man

Dear Fairy Man,

Please come and take me somewhere I need to go soon.

Love,
Annamae

Before sealing and mailing this letter, she illustrated it. Danny watched as she crayoned a figure with dark curly hair and a huge curly beard and a long apple green gown.

"What's that cigar-looking thing?" asked Danny, stirring his chocolate milk.

"A boat."

"Where do you need to go?"

Annamae drew blue water around the boat.

"Where do you want him to take you?"

She added some grass at the bottom.

"Where—"

"I haven't decided yet."

Danny swigged the milk, then burped deep and slow with his mouth open. "What about wings?"

"What?"

"Don't fairies have wings?"

Annamae pulled out her bottom lip and studied her drawing. After a long moment, she added wings.

Dollhouse

For her sixth birthday, Annamae was given a dollhouse. It was blue, with a yellow roof, and it had a handle so you could carry it around. The house opened on its hinges so you could see inside the rooms. There was a little doorbell you could really ring, and a garage door that really slid up and down. Some of the furniture was painted on the walls and some of it was real. When you closed the house and picked it up by the handle, you could hear the pieces of plastic furniture clunk around inside.

The dollhouse was the one Annamae's mother had played with when she was little. Not the same kind; the same exact one. She had gone over it with a warm soapy sponge before presenting it to Annamae, but you could still see traces of its earlier life as another child's toy. The child that Annamae's mother had once been had scribbled a picture in permanent marker on the wall of one of the bedrooms. Or she'd tried to and given up, or possibly she'd been found and stopped in the act—only two sides of the picture frame and a crossed-out something inside it had been completed. The child that Annamae's mother had once been had affixed some amazingly adhesive stickers—a kitten and a bicycle—to the outside of the house, over the rose trellis. They were still there all these years later, even though it looked like someone had tried to scrub them off.

"It's a real heirloom," said Nana when Annamae took the dollhouse to Nana's house across the river. "But what happened to all the people?"

"What people?"

"The family."

It had come with little plastic people, a mother and father and girl and boy, and a little plastic dog. Annamae's mother had bathed these, too, in warm soapy water, and she'd rolled each one up in a separate piece of tissue paper, twisting the ends like candy wrappers. On the morning of her birthday, Annamae had unwrapped them one by one.

Now she did not answer. She lay on her stomach on the plush carpet in Nana's living room and moved the furniture around, whispering all the while.

So Annamae's mother answered for her. "She's not into dolls."

"Whyever not?" said Nana.

The silence glowed. Annamae knew her mother was shrugging or making a face or maybe mouthing something to Nana on the couch.

"Then who's she talking to?" asked Nana, but she, too, had dropped her voice to a whisper.

Annamae grew fat with the warmth of being discussed.

It was true. She did not like dolls. They had no life. You were supposed to pretend they had. It was somehow a sign of being good—to care for dolls. Baby dolls especially. You were supposed to cradle and kiss them, scold and soothe them, hold a toy bottle against their rigid sculpted lips, wrap them in blankets and sing them lullabies. But when you laid them down to sleep, their arms remained sticking out, their little fingers remained stiffly crooked, and they did not cry or fuss.

Dolls had no choice but to obey. There was no possibility in dolls; they were lonely company.

What Annamae liked was the dollhouse itself. It held something beyond her control. A kind of puzzle. She sensed it in the half picture scribbled on the nursery wall, in the faded stickers that still clung to the rose trellis. They were like messages left by the slightly wayward child who would one day become her mother. It was to her, this distant child, that Annamae whispered as she rearranged pieces of furniture, pressed the working doorbell, and walked her fingers over the floors that some version of her mother, that faraway little girl, had also once touched.

Real

"Did you get in trouble?" Annamae asked her mother about scribbling on the dollhouse in permanent marker.

"I don't remember," her mother said.

"Did she?" Annamae asked Nana.

"Oh honey." Nana let out a breath that ruffled her lips. "Who knows?"

As if they were talking about other people, other lives.

The lingering presence of her mother's long-ago self was much more interesting to Annamae than the dolls that had come with the house. This appealingly somewhat naughty specter had more in common with the figures in the beehive office building, those milling silhouettes who kept her company on dark afternoons when she was sick, than with the tiny molded plastic dolls she could make do her bidding, marching them around the rooms of the dollhouse.

Suddenly, on her stomach on Nana's carpet, Annamae had a realization. It was about the story game. Whenever she played, whenever she whisper-narrated the happenings that unfolded across the street, it was every time the figures did *not* follow her instructions that counted as winning. The game's excitement lay in the tension of not knowing whether their actions would match her words or deviate from them. But the game's pleasure lay in their power to disobey.

It was because these figures were real that she felt a connection.

By real, she meant creatures not of her own making. Beyond her control.

Realer

"Do we ever get to the world that's realer than this?" Annamae wanted to know.

"What do you mean?" replied her mother.

She had just gotten picked up from ballet. Now the two of them were hurrying the seven blocks uptown to collect Danny from T-shirt Basketball at the Y. Her mother was threading so swiftly along the crowded sidewalk that Annamae had to do an extra skip every few steps in order not to fall behind. Her tights were sagging a little in the crotch, but there wasn't time to stop and pull them up. "Like, I know this world is real," she tried to explain, panting a bit, "but I mean a *realer* world."

"Yes, Annamae, I hear you; I'm just not understanding what you mean." Her mother was sounding a touch exasperated.

Annamae knew the feeling.

"Why do we always have to walk so fast?"

"Because we're always late."

"Why do we always have to be late?"

"Don't get me started."

At the corner, the light was, thankfully, against them. Annamae had time to pull up her tights and try again. "Like, the world that's just beyond—Mom, you're not even looking. Look!" She was holding up her hand, palm out, as a kind of visual aid. "Like that thing of how you can feel there's something just on the other side"—she pointed to the space on the far side of her palm—"*that* close, but you can't see it—Mom, look, look!"

"I am looking. What? I see."

Hopefully: "You do?"

"I see your hand."

The light changed.

"Let's go," said her mother, forging ahead.

In ballet today, they had been doing jetés, which were a way of jumping prettily with their legs and arms stretched out. But Ms. Jules had gotten mad—or not mad, serious—and made them stop. She had clapped her hands together and said, "No no no! You are making shapes. Do not just make shapes with your bodies—really reach!" They'd all tried again, stretching their legs and arms out even longer, but Ms. Jules had said, "No no no no! Not like you are grabbing for the jar of peanut butter!" This had made them laugh, but Ms. Jules did not laugh. She pressed pause on the music and gathered them around. "When you dance," she told them, pronouncing the words as if they were stamped in gold, "it is not about executing the steps, making the shapes. It is about reaching for something. Yes? It is a form of listening. Yes?"

Baffled, embarrassed, the students remained still.

"You must be," Ms. Jules told them, "like insects."

"Ew," somebody said.

"Like butterflies," she amended, "with antennae"—she placed her index fingers up by her temples—"always reaching, listening, feeling for something. A message, perhaps, on the wind."

Some of the children crooked their own index fingers up by their foreheads.

"A butterfly," Ms. Jules had continued, "is beautiful, yes. But a butterfly is not concerned with beauty. It is concerned only with the search."

The other children, wiggling their antennae, giggled,

but Annamae had felt something tighten in her spine. She did not know what Ms. Jules meant by *search*. But the thought—the wish—came into her mind that she might be on a search, too.

Now on the sidewalk, heading toward the Y, hop-skipping to keep up, frustrated and lonely because she had not been able to translate her question into language her mother, the linguist, could understand, she caught sight of her scurrying self reflected in a shop window. There was something about shop-window reflections that was always unsettling. The partialness of it, the way you could at once see yourself and see through yourself.

Annamae practiced a jeté, looking sideways at her reflection. There in the plate glass, leaping in parallel, part light, part shadow: an answering streak.

"Please don't dally," called her mother.

But she had to do one more, this time facing the shop window. So that she and her mirror self, as they leapt, each reached toward the other.

Coco

For her seventh birthday, Annamae received a blank book. It had a soft leather binding the color of cinnamon and a rawhide strap wound around its middle. She had been given diaries before: There had been one with a tiny lock and key, and before that one with a pink fur cover. But this book wasn't called a diary. It was a notebook. She corrected people if they got it wrong.

She took it with her most places: to the kitchen, to the bathroom, to her mother's room, to Danny's room. To school, to the park, to friends' apartments. To the dentist when she got her teeth cleaned, to the movies, the library, judo, ballet. Just anywhere. It accompanied her to meals (she'd put it under her thigh). It accompanied her to the playground (she'd ask whatever grown-up had brought her to hold it).

When Nana got them all tickets to see a shadow-puppet show, Annamae took it there, too.

Before the show began, a man came out onstage and explained that in his tradition, puppets are brought to life by the puppeteer, who is called (here he bowed) the Shadow Master. He'd brought one of the puppets, made of leather and carved like lace, and showed the audience how its arms and legs and even its jaw were jointed and attached to sticks. "Although I control the sticks," said the Shadow Master, taking another small bow, "in my tradition the puppets are not objects. They are spiritual beings." He explained that they were always kept upright, and given offerings (this made Annamae suck in her breath) "of sweets and flowers."

During intermission, they went to stretch their legs, and Annamae and Danny played a game of trying to get from one end of the lobby to the other without stepping on any of the paisley patterns on the carpet. Their minds were full of the tinkly music and the intricate shapes of the puppets, and they tried to replicate with their human limbs the movements of those jointed silhouettes. Annamae, who was of course doing all this with her notebook in hand, overheard Nana say, "Why did you let her bring her diary to the theater?"

"It's not her diary," she heard her mother say. "It's her transitional object."

"It's not my transipital object!" Annamae sang from across the lobby. She stroked its leather cover. She was already planning to give it offerings of sweets and flowers when they got home. "It's my company!"

It really was. After this, she stopped calling it her notebook and called it her company. Coco for short.

What a Planet

One Saturday when she was eight and Danny had just turned ten, they ate out in a coffee shop for the first time by themselves. They had gone with their mother to her office at the university's Child Language Lab. The plan was for them to play or read quietly for half an hour until Danny's friend Dante's dad could pick them up for T-shirt Basketball at the Y. But Dante's dad texted to say sorry he couldn't do it because Dante was having a reaction to a tree nut, so the kids were going to have to stay at the language lab for three whole hours, and they hadn't brought activities to fill three whole hours. So their mother said she would take them to the new coffee shop downstairs and see if they would allow the kids to stay by themselves while she finished up what she needed to do in the office.

The coffee shop was called Memuzin, and the man there was named Wasim. Wasim said, "Sure, sure. No problem, no problem. I have a daughter myself this age." Their mother gave him her phone number, and she gave Danny a ten-dollar bill, and then she hesitated and gave him another ten-dollar bill, and smiled at everyone quickly, one of her anxious flicker-smiles with the dent between her eyebrows, and then the kids stood watching the back of her gray wool coat disappear and listening to the bell attached to the door, which kept jingling after she was out of sight.

Wasim said, "Hey, hey, kids. Whatever you want. You let me know."

So Danny and Annamae went to the counter, where

each took a paper menu to study. Annamae practiced tendus while she read. Eventually, Danny ordered falafel and chocolate milk and Annamae ordered a bagel and hibiscus tea.

"You don't even know what that is," said Danny.

"Yes," said Annamae, going into elevé.

"How do you know?"

"This is when you're being so annoying, Danny."

"No, but how?"

He was good at being annoying, but Annamae was good at being silent.

Having their pick of tables, they sat at the one nearest the window. Annamae stuck Coco under her thigh and thought how terrible it would be if all the company she had was Danny.

Wasim brought their food and drinks. Annamae's tea was in a glass cup, on a glass saucer, and it was the red of cough syrup. Danny looked like he was trying not to appear jealous. It was steaming hot, so she dipped her spoon in to taste it. It wasn't any good, but there was a dish of sugar packets on the table. She stirred in five packets, and by then it was cool enough and sweet enough to drink.

Outside, the clouds that had been massing all morning turned sooty and jagged, and all the awnings started whipping, and in a matter of seconds it went from not raining to a downpour. It looked like someone was flinging handfuls of pearls on the asphalt and against the coffee shop window. Wasim came out from behind the counter and stood watching with them, his hands on his hips. When they turned to look at him, he just grinned and shook his head, as if to say, What a planet! The downpour lasted only a few minutes. Then it turned into regular rain, and Wasim went back behind the counter, and Annamae and Danny ate their food and drank their drinks and watched the cars go through the sudden puddles and send up crashing wings of water. It became a kind of game, waiting for cars to go through. They didn't say anything; it just became a game without their talking about it. They each knew the other was rooting for the same thing. Finally a bus came down the avenue and it went through a puddle and flung up a wave so big that it lashed against their window, and the two of them looked at each other with so much glee.

Soon after that, their mother came back to get them, unexpectedly early and with a real smile. "I had a cancellation, so that's it—we're done for the day." She still let Danny be the one to pay, using the two ten-dollar bills she'd given him. She watched him do all the math himself and count out the tip, and then they left, and it wasn't until they were almost home on the subway that Annamae realized she didn't have Coco.

Etiology

Tears, petitions, tantrums, contrition, repetition of petitions, but still their mother said no. Danny first argued passionately on Annamae's behalf ("Why not? We can just cross the platform and ride back uptown!"), then switched to reasoning with Annamae ("You can wait till Monday. No robber's going to want it."), then lost his patience ("Why do you have to be such a baby?"). When they got home their mother called Memuzin and spoke with Wasim, who located the leather book with the thong around its middle on the chair where Annamae had been sitting, and promised to keep it by the cash register until Monday. "And p-promise not to look inside!" said Annamae through hiccoughing sobs. She was tucked in a ball on the couch, on her side, heels against her bottom, hands around her ankles.

She refused supper. Afterward their mother came back to the couch, where Annamae now lay unfolded. Her mother noticed how long she had become: Her feet extended onto the third cushion. Settling herself onto that cushion and transferring Annamae's feet onto her lap, she said, "Feeling a little better?" Annamae said, "Worse." Danny said, "Give me a break," but their mother leaned over and touched Annamae's brow, first with her palm and then with the back of her hand. She said, "Huh," and brought the thermometer.

Annamae's temperature climbed in the night. By morning, even with Tylenol, it was 102.1. The pediatrician diagnosed an ear infection and sent them home with a prescription.

"There's absolutely no scientific basis for it," said their mother that afternoon, bringing a tray to Annamae, who lay in her mother's bed with its scent of apricot hand cream. The tray held the thermometer, more Tylenol, a tiny cup of thick pink medicine, a normal cup of ginger ale, a bowl of purple applesauce, and half a microwaved onion wrapped in a wool sock.

"The onion?" said Danny, who'd come along to witness the patient's reaction to the applesauce. The food coloring had been his contribution. "We know, we know."

"Actually," said their mother, "I was talking about the etiology."

"What's that?"

"The cause. I've never known anyone who could contract an ear infection from grief."

Annamae, even in her misery, could not help beaming weakly with pride.

Kiss

They had an Uncle Hersh, who was not really their uncle, but some kind of cousin. He had to be kissed. Whenever he came to their apartment, once a year or so, he would come after her, calling, "Where's Annamae? Annamae, where's my kiss?"

Annamae hoped that showing she was politely shy would get her off the hook, but no one helped—they only egged him on. His wife, Aunt Marni, would say, "Oh, Hersh, let her alone," with a fond shake of her head.

When she was cornered, he would put his hands behind his back and stoop—he was very tall—and she would have to kiss his cheek—soft and warm and slightly damp, like a hard-boiled egg—and he would straighten again, smiling, as if to say, I won, his lips sewed up tight against his rather jutting bite. Then he would wheel about and pay her no attention for the rest of the seder or Hanukkah party or Memorial Day or whatever it was. And her mouth would fill with foul-tasting saliva that she'd have to hold until she could dribble it onto a tissue.

When Annamae practiced kissing her self in the mirror, the sensation was hard and cool.

One year when Uncle Hersh came taunting and teasing—"Annamae? Where are you? Where's my kiss?"—and cornered her in the kitchen, before Annamae could give him his kiss, her mother said sharply, as if she'd already told Annamae a number of times, "I need you to take the garbage out *now*," and she stuck out the kitchen garbage bag, the dent between her eyebrows very deep. It was all so unjust. Annamae took the bag and slunk away down the stairs and put it in the metal can on the sidewalk. Her indignation mixed with a slithering shame. As if she really had been shirking.

Only in bed that night did Annamae realize what her mother had been up to. She felt a belated rush of gratitude. Seconds later, indignation set back in. Why, if her mother had meant to rescue her, did she have to mask it behind a scolding? Then she became curious. Why was it some things could be communicated outright, while others had to be in code?

And what was it about a kiss, anyway, that Uncle Hersh wanted one?

She got up and went to the bathroom, found the tube of lipstick that had lived for years in the medicine cabinet, and rubbed it thickly over her mouth. Back in her room, she took Coco from her bedside table, opened to a fresh page, and kissed it. She studied the resulting blotch. Disappointingly indecipherable—you couldn't even tell what it was meant to be.

Cleft

Annamae's bed was a piece of foam rubber resting on a piece of plywood resting on five cans of whole peeled tomatoes, the thirty-five-ounce size. Danny had the exact same bed in his room across the hall.

Their mother and father had moved into this apartment before the kids existed (Danny liked to say that in actual point of fact they'd *existed;* it was just that at that time they'd been divided, residing half in their mother and half in their father). Their mother had been studying psycholinguistics and working as a lab assistant, and their father had been writing a play and working as a pizza deliverer. Their furniture was mostly hand-me-downs and things that had been put out on the curb. Their bed was a queen-size piece of foam rubber resting on twin plywood panels resting on ten cans of tomatoes. When Danny and Annamae were ready to move out of their cribs, a friend with an electric carving knife came over and sliced the foam rubber down the middle. Cleft it in two.

"That's a contranym, you know," their mother said.

"What's a contranym?"

"A word with two opposite meanings. You can cleave a bed in two"—she made a chopping motion with her hand—"or I can cleave you to my bosom"—she drew Annamae against her body.

Annamae slipped the embrace. "Who was the friend?"

"Freddie Festano."

"Who's *that?*"

"Your father knew him from playing ball."

They knew all about their father's basketball prowess. They often walked by the very courts where he had played pickup games. They liked to stand with their faces almost touching the fence and observe the people who were not their father play on those same courts now. Annamae would watch them crouching and panting and pausing and dashing, slapping the ball away from the net or scooping it in, and think about how sometimes they must be stepping into the exact same spaces their father's body had once occupied. She liked to think something happened at those moments of perfect overlap, that a little chime went off somewhere. She thought of it as the sharp, short *ping* of the dollhouse doorbell. She'd stand there thinking, Now. Now. Now. Now. Watching them lift their T-shirts to wipe their slick faces. Though most of the time they just let their sweat flow, impressive amounts of it dripping like rain from their jaws, wrists, even their knees.

"Let's invite him for dinner."

"I haven't been in touch with him in a million years," said their mother. "I'm surprised I remembered the name."

"Why did he have an electric carving knife?" Danny wanted to know.

"Well." Their mother looked stumped. "For turkey, I guess."

"What did you sleep on then?"

"The bed I have now," said their mother. They watched her stroke her imaginary mustache. Her voice grew wondering, as if the next thing she said came from a poem: "We bought it new."

Annamae wrote the name Freddie Festano in her leather book. A whole section of Coco was for nothing but names, names collected from real life and from books and from her imagination.

Lying in bed, she thought of when it had been one with Danny's bed. One piece of foam.

She thought of when it had been their parents' bed, and then their father had died, and she and Danny outgrew their cribs, and Freddie Festano came over with his electric carving knife.

She thought of Freddie Festano shooting a basket with his electric carving knife sticking out of his pocket.

She thought of the men on the basketball court. Their amazing sweat, so gross and impressive. Their shining necks, their hairy shins.

She thought of the way whenever her mouth touched Uncle Hersh's cheek she had to hold her saliva until she could spit into a tissue.

She thought of kissing her reflection in the mirror. The sensation of being joined, cleaved for that moment, to the girl that was not-her.

Penny Game

For one entire year, their babysitter after school four days a week was Nobomi, one of their mother's grad students. She was from South Africa and spoke isiXhosa—she was doing research in the language lab on how babies make the click sounds—and she taught Annamae and Danny a nursery rhyme called "*Umzi watsha*" about a house on fire. She made them sun butter and frozen banana sandwiches, took them to judo and ballet and T-shirt Basketball, painted their toenails, gave them an ant farm, listened to them tell their whole dreams. She was the best babysitter they'd ever had, and when she got strep and Nana had to substitute, they were horrified.

"Oh please," their mother said. "You kids are beyond spoiled."

"But, Mom"—they tried to soften their criticism by gesturing extravagantly with their hands and eyebrows—"we love Nana. It's just she's no good at taking care of kids."

"Hello," said their mother, waving hello. "She took care of this kid." Pointing at herself.

"It's just she's no good at taking care of *us*."

Their mother stopped walking and gave them her "We are not amused" look. She had taught them about the *pluralis majestatis,* otherwise known as the royal *we*.

"Can I be the one to put it in?" asked Annamae. They had come to their destination, the corner mailbox. It had been many years since Annamae played her post office game with the accordion radiator in the corner of the kitchen.

Some of her old mail still lived back there, beneath the dust bunnies and cobwebs.

"Then I get to hold it open," said Danny. So their mother gave Annamae the manila envelope with the get well cards and drawings they had made for Nobomi and Danny pulled open the blue metal door, then pretended he was going to shut it on Annamae's hand. She cried out in surprise; he laughed; she slapped him; he shoved her; she cried out again; their mother said, "I'm so glad I chose to have children"; and they all tramped home in foul moods.

It turned out to be an okay time with Nana. She was more strict and less fun than Nobomi, but less strict and more fun than they remembered. She let them make her a sun butter and frozen banana sandwich, which she declared "a revelation." And she taught them a game called Penny. It was kind of dumb. All it was was this: They would go for a walk together, and each time they reached an intersection, they would take turns flipping a penny and letting the penny decide which way to go. Heads was right and tails was left. There was never any fighting, because everything was up to the penny. And it was surprisingly exciting, because everything was up to the penny. Which meant, if you took the game seriously, you might wind up very far from home by suppertime. If you took the game really, really seriously, Danny pointed out, you might never get home, ever.

Annamae thought about this. She had to stop walking and work it out by drawing an imaginary route with her finger on her palm. Seeing that he was right, she looked at Nana, who was proceeding unconcernedly down the block. In her mauve windbreaker, white sneakers, and little nylon bag clipped around her waist, she looked like she could go for a long time.

Coco! thought Annamae, wondering if it was too late to run back and get her leather companion.

"Keep up," called Danny over his shoulder, and after another moment's hesitation, she ran to catch up.

They got home that night after dark. Their mother greeted them with annoyance and relief. She had already taken the tuna noodle casserole out of the oven. "*And* dressed the salad," she told Nana accusingly.

Over supper they all took turns telling about their adventure, how they'd almost ended up in the Holland Tunnel, how in one spot the penny kept being tails and they had to go around and around the same block, how once Annamae dropped the penny and it had nearly rolled into the hole in a sewer cover.

"Then we would never have gotten back," declared Nana.

And although Annamae knew Nana didn't really mean it, for a long time after, whenever she saw a vented sewer cover, she'd think of the penny. She'd picture it—with its power to determine where she would go—dropping through the hole to the other side, flipping over and over as it fell.

Letter Game

Their mother was going to Zagreb for five days for a conference called Linguistic and Nonlinguistic Interactional Synchrony.

"What's Zagreb?"

It was the capital of Croatia.

"What's international symphony?"

"Inter*actional synchr*ony. It's actually super interesting. It's how a baby and its mother, or really any two people, but especially a baby and mother, when they're really in sync, tend to mirror each oth—"

"What about us?"

Danny and Annamae would stay at Nana's.

"Why can't Nobomi take care of us?"

She was going to the conference, too.

"Do we have to go to Nana's? Her house smells like a waiting room."

That was just furniture polish.

"But why can't she stay here?"

It was too many days.

"If it's too many days for her to stay here, then isn't it too many days for us to have to go there?"

Kids were more adaptable.

"How do you know?"

"I've been one," their mother replied.

They wound up having a good time at Nana's. It was their spring break. They went to the library, where the children's room had beanbag chairs and an enormous fish tank. They walked to the ferry landing and watched the ferries dock and depart. They did a science experiment. Nana poured a glass of seltzer and told them each to put in a raisin. The raisins sank to the bottom, where they collected bubbles, rose to the surface where the bubbles popped, and sank again, over and over. ("Mine's beating yours," said Danny. "It's not a race," said Annamae. "It's science," said Nana.)

And she taught them how to make icebox cake. That was a little like science, too. All you did was whip cream, use it to glue thin chocolate cookies together in rows, put the plate in the fridge, and take it out after dinner. As Nana said, Presto! Somehow the crisp wafers turned into chocolate sponge.

They slept in their mother's old bedroom, Danny in the twin bed and Annamae on a roll-out cot. The room had rosebud wallpaper and a pink dresser and a small white vanity with a pink upholstered stool. It seemed to have nothing to do with their mother. Annamae tried to imagine the girl her mother had once been living in this room. The first night, after Nana tucked them in and turned off the lights, Annamae cried.

"Are you homesick?" asked Danny.

"Yes."

"Do you want to play the letter game?"

"Yes."

He lifted his covers and moved over to make room.

She got in beside him and lay on her stomach.

Danny's finger traced shapes on her back.

"C . . ." read Annamae. "*A . . . N . . .*"

"No. I'll do it again."

"*F?*"

"No. Concentrate."

"*K?*"

"Yeah."

"E. Cake?"

"Yeah. My turn." Danny turned onto his stomach, and Annamae thought of a word to spell.

Later, when she was drifting off, Danny gave her a nudge. "Can you get back in your own bed now?"

So she returned to the cot, and fell asleep with letters in her head.

The Alphabet

It wasn't only the leather book with the thong around the middle that provided Annamae with company. It was the messages she wrote in it, messages to someone, or no one. To no one she'd met, but someone she felt—trusted—was intimately connected with her. She had a feeling that one day they'd be meeting up, or else they'd already met in some distant past, and it was this feeling, perhaps, that kept her company.

Because she wasn't sure what form of communication was best suited to such a connection, she experimented. She wrote variously with pencil or colored pencil or crayon or ballpoint pen or felt-tip marker or even (once when she'd gotten a paper cut) with her own thumbprint in blood. Sometimes she drew pictures or sketched maps, like when she'd traced the route they'd taken on the penny game. Sometimes she glued in artifacts, like the flower petals she'd collected, inspired by the shadow-puppet show, to give Coco as an offering. Sometimes she wrote real words, and sometimes nonsense combinations of letters. One whole section was dedicated to the alphabet, page upon page where she recorded each letter and all its attributes: color, personality, age, hobbies, siblings, favorite food, gender. Some letters were very definitely girl or boy, some contained aspects of both, and some had no gender at all.

When she was little and just learning how to form letters, she'd had strong convictions about how her own name was meant to be written. For example, it was clear to her that capital *E* consisted of one vertical line to which a person was meant to attach as many horizontal lines as felt right on any given occasion. Sometimes this resulted in four horizontals, sometimes seven. Danny tried to tell her this was silly, but how could it be silly in a world where losing teeth and growing new teeth was normal?

For another example, it was clear to her that *e*, kelly green, was the smiliest of letters and therefore she liked to make it large, whereas *m*, the color of silverware, was stern to the point of disapproving, and so was best rendered quite little. *A* was the most serene of the letters; both wise and dreamy, it was the color of blue chalk. And *n*, which could be either black or white, was the most helpful. It had the disposition of a school nurse.

Additionally, because it was evident to her that the second *n* in her name performed no useful role in its assigned spot, she experimented with moving it around, sometimes moving it up front: Nanamae; sometimes bumping it over one place: Ananmae; sometimes trying it down near the end: Anamane; and sometimes, most audaciously, not only moving the second *n* but adding a third: Anamanen. For the rest of her life, her mother would, from time to time, resurrect that last variation, calling her in moments of affectionate amusement Anamanen, or rather, Anomenon, to rhyme with *phenomenon*.

The Alef-bet

They had finished lunch at the wooden picnic table that was their kitchen table and moved to the living room part of the room. Rav Harriett was sitting in the brown armchair, her mother was sitting in the blue armchair, and Annamae was sitting on the floor between them with her drawing pad and her box of pencils, crayons, and markers. Danny was somewhere. Rav Harriett was wearing stockings and low high heels. She was older than their mother, although it was difficult to say how old, because it seemed like she came from an older time period. She always sat with her ankles crossed, and Annamae liked the sound her stockings made whenever she uncrossed them and crossed them the other way. The grown-ups were drinking tea with milk in it and having a conversation with lots of words in it that Annamae didn't know, and Annamae was drawing a picture of their conversation:

yes
no
yes
no
yes
yes
no
yes
no
no
no

At some point the conversation paused, and Annamae felt Rav Harriett leaning forward, studying her paper. The sensation of being studied was a feather stroking her neck.

"Are you writing a poem?" asked Rav Harriett.

"No," said Annamae. "I'm drawing a picture."

"Er . . . what's that a picture of?" This was her mother, openly amused.

"Of your guys' conversation."

Annamae could feel them exchanging a look. She knew it was a look of *Oh, how we love Annamae!* but she felt it called for some correction. She made her neck very long for dignity as she explained, "The yeses are when you're saying things I can understand and the nos are when you use words I don't know."

"And what are the letters along the edges?" asked Rav Harriett. Her voice had the best rough, low, watery scratchiness to it. It was like biting into a sour pickle.

"Those are—those, you see, those are the moods." Annamae felt her face grow warm with the effort of explaining something so private. "This *yes* is friendly and bouncy, this *yes* is kind but very tired, this *no* is goofy, and this *no* has its arms folded across its chest." She showed them, folding her own arms across her chest. Her mother was smiling like *What a pip my daughter is!* but Rav Harriett had a look on her face that was only vaguely a smile. It was a look of *Wait—have we met?*

She asked Annamae to tell her more.

"Well," said Annamae, "that word you said before? There was a word you said, like *dapple-gangle?* I don't know. But anyway, that's this *no* and it goes with this dark-green *w* and this violet *j*. Because it sort of has the feeling of a cave in the forest in the winter in the middle of the night?" And tracing her finger across the page like her mother used to do when she was little and they read picture books together, Annamae gave Rav Harriett a guided tour of all the letters she'd made along the border, explaining what their different colors meant and which yeses and nos they went with. As she spoke, the feeling of dignity came upon her more and more. It reminded her of the time Ms. Jules had told the ballet class about butterflies and antennae and dance being about listening for something that wasn't there more than about making pretty shapes, and how some of the children had giggled, but she, Annamae, had felt a grave, solemn thing bloom along her spine.

"Did you know, Annamae," said Rav Harriett when she had finished, "that there are people, sages, who believe the letters of the Hebrew alphabet all have special personalities and meanings?" She sounded like she had just done some jumping jacks.

Annamae shook her head no. She felt a little out of breath, too.

The following day, Rav Harriett came over again. Usually they saw her maybe a couple times a year. But this time she came back the very next day, late in the afternoon, with a present for Annamae: a pale brown booklet for practicing how to write the letters of the Hebrew alphabet. Only it wasn't called the alphabet, Rav Harriett explained. It was called the *alef-bet*.

"Don't worry, Jo, I'm not here to convert anybody," Rav Harriett told Annamae's mother as Annamae sat at the wooden picnic table and bent her head over the book.

"Please. Do I look worried?" Annamae's mother had been stirring spaghetti sauce in one pot on the stove and bringing water to a boil in another. Now she took an extra plate from the cupboard.

"Nor am I here to mooch dinner—why are you setting another place? Stop. Jo. Annamae, tell your mother to stop."

Danny came pounding up the stairs, smelling of basketball and the cold. "Hi, Harriett," he said. He had missed her entirely on her visit the day before. Months had passed since they'd seen each other.

"My God," said Rav Harriett, looking up at him even though she was wearing her low high heels. "What percentile is this child in?"

Their mother just shook her head and smiled, doing all different things at once: spaghetti, carrots, napkins, butter, candles.

"What's that?" Danny asked, dropping onto the wooden bench close beside Annamae.

"You're all sweaty," she said.

"I know."

"Yuck, Danny."

Danny just pushed his sweaty hair off his forehead and watched as she first traced with her pencil and then copied the form of the *alef* over and over on the lines left blank for that purpose. "What is it?" he asked again.

Annamae looked up at Rav Harriett with a face that said, *You explain.*

Four Stories

There was a tradition that the letters of the *alef-bet* have a life beyond pencil and paper, Rav Harriett told them. "A life beyond language, even," she added, peeping pointedly over the top of her gold-rimmed glasses at their mother.

Their mother, the linguist, made a face like *Who am I to argue with a rabbi?*

Then Rav Harriett told them four stories about the life of the letters of the *alef-bet*.

The first was about creation. It said that in the beginning God began to play, for delight's sake, with the signs and wonders ("That's what we now call letters," Rav Harriett said). God shaped them and mixed them and rearranged them and tossed them from hand to hand and pretty soon they began to flow and whirl and dance and lo! From them everything came into being.

The second story was about Moses. It said that when he got angry and threw down the tablets that had the Ten Commandments written on them, the tablets themselves shattered and lay on the ground, but the letters that had been carved on them? The letters flew up to heaven.

The third was about a shepherd boy. This boy wanted to pray, but he didn't know how to read the prayer book. So he said to God, "I'll just call out all the letters and You, You go ahead and arrange them in the way that pleases You most!" And God really liked this.

The last story she told them was more obscure. ("What's obscure?" they wanted to know. By then the spaghetti was bubbling in the pot and the windowpanes over the sink as well as the lenses of her glasses had become fogged. "Not well known," said Rav Harriett. "More literally, hidden," put in their mother, the linguist.) This was the story that one letter is missing from the *alef-bet*. It was there in the beginning, but it got lost. "Only," said Rav Harriett, "when it is found will the brokenness in the universe be healed."

Gravity Game

"When will I have a friend?" asked Annamae.

"You have friends," said her mother, and proceeded to name them.

Annamae emitted a sound between a whimper and a scoff. "Not like that." She was lying the wrong way on the couch, her legs going up the back cushion, her upper body hanging off the seat so her head nearly touched the floor. She was playing what she called "the gravity game." It involved being upside down long enough that gravity reversed. By now, the floor had fully become the ceiling and the ceiling had fully become the floor. If she wanted to get up and look out the window, she'd have to walk across the ceiling to get there.

"I guess I'm not understanding what you mean." Her mother was sitting in the blue armchair, holding a purple-and-orange book and wearing her green readers. All these colors were simply amazing, viewed upside down. They should have different names, these colors. That's how different they looked from the other side of gravity.

"A *friend*," enunciated Annamae, hauling herself back into sitting position. The room spun giddily.

Her mother looked at her, not without sympathy. But perhaps with a fairly limited amount.

"A *FRIEND*."

"Yes, I heard you. I'm just not catching the connotation." Maddeningly, her mother went back to her reading.

A Friend. A Friend. A Friend. A Friend. Annamae said

it over and over in her head until it became nothing but a sound stripped of meaning. But what she meant did have meaning. It's just that there wasn't a word for it. Or if there was, it remained obscure. Hidden. Like the missing letter of the *alef-bet*.

She kneaded her foot, which had pins and needles, which Danny had once explained to her was because of blood rushing back into the part of your body where it had been temporarily cut off. A little fury built up in her. Little pointy flames. Everything in this house had to be explained away by science.

"It's not *science,*" grumbled Annamae.

Her mother gave no sign of having heard.

"What if my Friend doesn't live in this world?" she said a little louder.

"What world do you think she lives in?" Her mother turned a page.

"What if my Friend doesn't live in this same time?"

Mildly, abstractedly, her mother suggested, "Why don't you write her a letter?"

"Mom! That's so stupid! How would I even mail it?"

Now her mother did look up. "I'm sorry, Annamae," she said coldly. "I guess I don't understand what you're saying." Then she went back to her book.

"What even is that?" yelled Annamae.

"What?"

"What you're reading."

"*The Journal of Child Language.*"

Annamae emitted a fantastically rude, incredulous squawk.

Dredging her gaze up from the page once more, her mother peered over the top of her readers in a way that meant *You wish to comment?*

"Guess they don't really know what they're talking about."

She watched her mother teeter along the edge of a decision. Whether to scold or to laugh. Maybe it was less a decision than an involuntary eruption. At any rate, a moment later, the two of them were in such hysterics, the kind of laughter that's both delicious and painful, that Danny came bounding down the stairs, demanding, "What? What's funny? Tell it to me, too!"

Still. Long after the hilarity died down, Annamae remained vexed. She could feel something lodged inside her, hard as a pebble. She knew what it was. A kind of longing.

Lipstick

Their apartment was a little broken. The windowpanes didn't quite fit their frames. Drafts got in, and soot. The crack across the kitchen wall had recently gotten bigger. And there was an actual hole in the floor of the upstairs hallway that looked right down onto the couch. It was not big enough for a penny, but you could push a Tic Tac through. Once, a bracelet Annamae had gotten as a party favor broke and she lay on her stomach and encouraged all the clear pink seed beads toward the hole. They rained down with a satisfying patter on the living room part of the downstairs. "Pennies from heaven," said her mother drily from the couch, where some of the pink beads landed.

"They're not pennies," called Annamae, one eye to the hole. "And this isn't heaven!"

"Idiom," said her mother.

To this day, you could still sometimes find one of the beads stuck between the cushions.

Also the apartment had crooked floors. In some of the rooms the floor slanted this way and in some of the rooms it slanted that way. In the kitchen, it managed to slant both ways.

The kids used this to their advantage when they were building marble runs. They knew just how to work with all the various slopes and dips to maximize speed and smoothness. "You're real connoisseurs of the topography," their mother remarked.

"What does that mean?" they wanted to know. They thought she was calling them a type of dinosaur.

But no, she explained. *Topography* meant the surface features of a place. And *connoisseurs,* she said, meant "You know these floors like the back of your hand."

At this, Annamae and Danny stopped putting together pieces of marble track and examined the backs of their hands. Annamae felt she did not know hers all that well. There was a little freckle or mole on one that she'd never noticed before. And some purple marker she didn't realize she had gotten on herself. Also her veins looked weird. The longer she studied them, the stranger her own hands looked.

Their mother told them a story about the crooked floors. When she and their father had been apartment hunting and they'd come to this one, their mother had liked it, but their father had said, "We can't live here; the floors are tilted."

"No they're not," their mother had said.

"Give me your lipstick," said their father.

So she handed him the tube of lipstick from her purse and he set it at his feet and it rolled straight across the room.

"So he was right," said Danny.

"He was."

"But you wound up here anyway."

"We did."

Then Danny didn't say anything else, although for several moments it looked like there was something else he wanted to say.

For Annamae, the most interesting part of the story was learning that their mother had once carried lipstick in her purse.

Signal

Smack beside their own front door, wooden and painted red, was another door made all of glass, and beside it a glass storefront. That was why they didn't have a first floor (except for the vestibule stuffed with umbrellas and boots and knapsacks and everything): They lived above a shop. When they were little, it had been a hardware store. Then it became a hair salon, then a dog salon, then a French bakery, and now it was a shop that sold nothing but lights. Danny missed the dog salon because he liked seeing the different sorts of dogs and how they got their fur shaped like, he said, the bushes in rich-people parks. Their mother missed the bakery, because in warm weather the smell of sugar and vanilla would climb right up into their open windows like, she said, the prince in Rapunzel. But Annamae loved the lighting shop, spangled floor to ceiling with different colors and shapes and sizes of lightbulbs and table lamps and floor lamps and pendants and chandeliers and track lights and string lights.

During the cold and dark part of the year especially, she loved rounding the corner from the avenue onto their street and seeing it, the shop beneath their home, lit like a ship on a dark sea. She felt safe whenever she saw that ship—or rather, that shop. She felt safe and at the same time she felt a kind of frantic ecstasy. That shop of lights, that storefront glowing in the gloom, in some strange, definite way sent her signals. As if the lights were a kind of language.

"Actually, lights can be used as language." So said her

mother when Annamae shyly communicated her feeling. It was both thrilling and deflating, the matter-of-factness of her mother's response. "For Morse code. Signal lights are still used, I think, by ships and airplanes."

"And trains," said Danny. "Even the subway—haven't you ever noticed?"

"Right," said their mother. "Not Morse code, but still a kind of language. For that matter—" She stopped in her tracks and pointed toward the intersection. They'd been to the park and were walking home. It was a blustery day, and the traffic light suspended high on its pole dangled like a leaf on its stem. They stood and watched as the big lit circle switched from yellow to red and the cars on the avenue stopped, and the cars on the street went forward, and all the people on the corners exchanged places with one another. Everyone fluent in light language, everyone in too much of a rush to notice.

The only ones not in a rush were Annamae and Danny and their mother. For them, time had slowed. A little island with their own tempo, they waited a full cycle for the signal to change again.

Somebody impatient to get somewhere brushed by them with a *tsk* as loud as a popped cork, then called back as if issuing a grand proclamation, "You're not the only ones in the world!"

Star

But it wasn't really that. It wasn't that the lights could be used as signals. It was more that they held messages.

One time they had been driving home from visiting Nana, who lived across the river in what was called a Dutch Colonial. After supper they had sat at the table playing Liverpool and smoking pretzel-rod cigars for a long time, so it was well after dark when they started home. Danny and their mother were talking up front and Annamae, lying on the backseat with her coat folded under her head, knew they assumed she had fallen asleep. She had not. She was looking, full of awakeness and curiosity, out the car window at a star, a single star that kept following them.

She usually did fall asleep on the drive home from Nana's, and, in fact, had changed into pajamas before they left, but for some reason this time the motion of the car hurtling through space, together with the vibration of the engine beneath her body, together with the lullaby concoction of familiar voices and indistinguishable words drifting from the front seat—these things did not ease her into sleep but instead seemed to be spinning a kind of bright pinwheel inside her chest.

The thought struck Annamae, watching that teeny diamond spur in the sky, keeping sight of it as it kept sight of her, that they were in conversation. She and the star. She didn't know exactly what they were saying to each other. It had the feeling of a promise, a vow. But it didn't matter—the content of the exchange was less important than her recognition of it. That, and understanding that it wasn't the first time she had found herself having such a dialogue. It wasn't new. If anything, it was a renewal.

She must have slept at some point. She didn't remember the moment she lost sight of the star, although she would have been parted from it in any case when they went through the tunnel. But once she was roused from the backseat by her mother's hand, once she let herself be coaxed grumpily back into her coat, once she'd shoved her feet back into her unlaced sneakers and was trudging sleepily toward home alongside her mother and Danny down the block from where they'd gotten a parking space, once she saw across the street the lighting shop radiating its good, indifferent welcome, she remembered the star. And looked for it in the narrow band of sky above the rooftops.

"Keep walking, honey. It's chilly and we're all tired."

The sky was so much busier here in the city than it was at Nana's. Its puffy glow got in the way. It was making the star—what was the word Rav Harriett taught them?—obscure.

"Come, please."

She went on tiptoe and swayed this way and that, trying to see beyond the zigzag of rooftops and the crowns of trees. There! Beyond the branches of a honey locust, she spotted it. Her diamond chip.

"Annamae."

She was almost sure it was the one.

Ferryman

A new place was opening at the end of their block, in the spot where Malachi's had always been.

Malachi's was a bar. Its official name was Malachi's Pub & Kitchen, spelled out in dark letters on a dirty awning, but their mother called it a bar, and she always got that little dent between her eyebrows whenever they had to step around the garbage bags piled up on the sidewalk out front. Danny and Annamae had forever wanted to try it out, the kitchen part, but their mother said they just served past-date hamburgers and extra-greasy fries. "How do you know, have you been without us?" the kids asked. Their mother said she could just tell.

One day both of Malachi's storefront windows were smashed. The next day the windows were boarded up with plywood, and over the awning was a bright blue sign saying FOR LEASE.

"What do you think will be there now? I hope it's another dog salon," said Danny.

"I hope it's another French bakery," said their mother.

"You wouldn't have the smells climbing in your window," pointed out Annamae. "It wouldn't be right beneath us."

"But just think—we'd have fresh croissants right down the block!"

"I wouldn't mind if it's a comic-book store," Danny went on. "Or a taqueria. Or an arcade. Or a tattoo parlor!"

Their mother swiveled her head. "Who *are* you?"

"What do you hope it is?" Danny asked Annamae.

"A lost and found."

He guffawed. "That's not a thing."

"Of course it is."

"Not as a store."

"It could be."

"That's not how it works. Mom, tell her."

"Danny!" The swift intensity of Annamae's rage came as a surprise to them all; her voice was sharp and slashing. "You don't get to tell me what I hope!"

Then one day the plywood vanished from Malachi's windows. In fact, the whole storefront was missing. You could look straight inside and see workers with power saws and lumber and stepladders and drywall. Instead of smelling like old beer and rancid oil, the place smelled like sawdust and fresh chemical-y newness. Over time, they saw it transform into a new establishment for eating and drinking—"Another bar," said their mother with a sigh—but cleaner and spiffier than Malachi's. They put in a black-and-white tiled floor and a marble bar top.

"Can we try eating at this one when it opens?" the kids asked.

"They'll serve thirty-dollar burgers and charge extra for fries."

"How do you know?"

"I can just tell."

At last it appeared ready to open. Where the dirty old awning had once hung, a new wooden sign got installed. They saw it for the first time on their way to school one morning.

"Oh," said Annamae, halting in her tracks. Gold letters on a black background spelled THE FERRYMAN.

"Come on," said Danny. They were running late.

"I know this place."

"Duh, we walk by it every day."

"No, I mean. I've known about him. I used to write him letters."

"Who?"

"The ferryman. Don't you remember?"

"No."

"You helped. When we used to play post office? With the radiator?"

She remembered what she had written him, too. *Dear Fairy Man, Please come and take me somewhere I need to go soon. Dear Fairy Man, How is your boat doing? I need you to bring me to the other side. Dear Fairy Man, Many times I have asked you, but you have not answered me.*

Now she realized this was what she had meant all along. Not Fairy Man, but Ferryman.

"Kids!" That was their mother, up ahead. The light had just changed. "Let's cross!"

Friends

Annamae had two main friends: Carla and Renu.

Carla had started as a problem. In first grade, the first time Annamae had gone to the bathroom all by herself, she'd been sitting on the toilet inside a stall when someone came into the bathroom and a girl started saying, "Who's in here? Who's in here?" and pushing the doors open one by one. When she got to Annamae's stall, Annamae had been relieved that the door stayed closed. But a moment later, the girl stuck her head under the door and there she was, lying on her stomach and looking up at Annamae, saying, "What's your name? Why you don't answer me?"

Annamae, whose feet didn't reach the ground, was swinging her legs back and forth a little bit, and her shoe touched the girl's nose.

"You kicked me!" said the girl.

"Sorry," whispered Annamae. Her heart was beating fast. Her underpants were striped white and mint green.

Then the door to the bathroom opened and a teacher's voice said, "Carla Watkins, what are you doing? Carla, get up off the ground," and the face withdrew and pretty soon the bathroom was empty and quiet, except for a fly that was buzzing against the window.

Carla was in a different class, but at recess Annamae saw her again, standing on the rubber jiggly bridge of the climbing structure. She was shaking it and shouting to some other kids, "Try to cross! Come on, try to get across!"

Annamae went over to her and said in a good strong voice, "My name is Annamae."

Carla turned. "Annamae!" She repeated her name like it was astounding. "Can I touch your hair?"

Annamae's mother had given her braids that morning.

Carla's touch was unexpectedly gentle. As if Annamae's head was a baby rabbit.

Renu had started as a responsibility. A month into second grade, the teacher stood at the front of the room with a new girl in a babyish blue dress with a white collar and said, "Who would like to be Renu's new-school buddy?" Annamae was one of several girls who shot up their arms. She was happy when the teacher picked her, and then a moment later, realizing this meant she would have to really do it, she felt a muddle of confused regret.

It turned out only Renu's dress was babyish, not her way of looking you in the eye when she spoke or listened to you speak, and not her handwriting, which was so beautiful, it gave Annamae a pang. She had moved from Pittsburgh, Pennsylvania, which, she explained, was nicknamed "Steel City," and she gave Annamae a souvenir piece of steel in a little red box. So Annamae gave Renu her best pencil, which was blue at one end and red at the other, and then she was sorry, because she loved that pencil. But the next day, Renu came wearing jeans and a velvet headband, and at lunch they traded: Renu's Nice Time biscuits for Annamae's Fig Newtons. Annamae confided that she liked Renu's handwriting, and Renu confided, "I'm mature for my age."

In third grade, the three of them got put into the same class. They knew they had become a real trio when Ms. Zmijewski wouldn't let them have desks near one another. Sometimes after school they all got picked up by Carla's babysitter, sometimes by Renu's grandparents, sometimes by Nobomi or Annamae's mother. On Thursdays after school, all three of them got signed up for Art Explorers, where they made potato prints, flip-books, cardboard tube skylines, and papier-mâché mythical beasts. On Valentine's Day Annamae gave Carla and Renu stained-glass cookies she'd made with Nana by shaping dough into the outline of a heart and baking them with crushed hard candies melted in the middle. "You hang them in the window." She showed them the loop of yarn she and Nana had tied through a hole in each cookie after it had cooled.

"You can't eat it?" Carla touched her tongue to a piece of candy glass.

"Well, you *can* . . ."

Carla bit in.

Renu, curling her fingers in a loose fist near her mouth, giggled. "Oh Carla!"

Doing her best Cookie Monster and spraying bits of crumb, Carla rumbled, "Me like!"

Friendship

Through it all, Annamae knew there was something else. A different sort of friendship, as different from her friendship with Carla and Renu as the ocean is different from a tear, never mind that both are salt water. She knew with great solemnity not just that a different sort of friendship was possible but also that it existed specifically for her. It was as if she'd been told about such a friendship a long time ago, and it was more than just a story: It was a promise. It was as if she'd peeked ahead in a book about herself and her eye had caught some words, a definite clue that such friendship was real, and awaited her even now. But how to reach it, how to get there? The friendship she sought seemed to lie on the other side of something. All she had to do was figure out a way to cross over.

She knew this as surely as if it was the message the lighting shop beneath their apartment beamed out to her whenever she came around the corner on a smoke-colored afternoon and saw it gleaming there, its table lamps and floor lamps and track lighting and chandeliers all lit and signifying something. She knew it as surely as if it was the message the star had been telling her that night they'd stayed late playing Liverpool at Nana's and she'd lain awake in the backseat and it, the pinprick hole, the grain of salt, the crumb of crystal in the sky, had kept her company all the way home.

Sometimes the pressure of this knowledge was almost unbearable.

The new bar at the end of their block felt like a signal that she was not wrong. She was on the right track; she was in the right neighborhood. She had only to be patient. Walking by the Ferryman, she could not help lingering to look inside, hoping to spot him, this figure she'd had in her mind since she'd been little. She'd know him when she saw him: a big man with a big black beard. He might or might not have wings.

"Stop that," Danny said one bright afternoon when she cupped her hands around her face and pressed her nose to the glass. "You look weird."

"What? You do it," said Annamae.

"At the pet shop. Not at a bar."

Sometimes it felt as if this unknown Friend longed for her as powerfully as she pined for the Friend, and then she wished she could deliver a message, could say reassuringly, "I'm here. I exist. I'm coming."

She wrote these words in the pages of Coco. Ever since almost losing the little leather book at Memuzin, she had stopped taking it with her everywhere. Now it mostly stayed on her bedside table, along with the pale brown booklet Rav Harriett had given her for practicing the letters of the *alef-bet,* and a four-color ballpoint pen Renu had given her for her ninth birthday.

Yes, she was nine now. And Coco was nearly full.

Stairs

Leslie at Art Explorers taught them how to make the stairs.

Leslie wore her locs tied up in colorful head wraps. She had big round glasses, and tattoos covering both arms. When they first started Art Explorers, they'd called her "Miss Leslie," but when they got to fourth grade they dropped the "Miss." It happened without their being told or asking permission. As if by some signal, they all just started calling her by her first name.

This session of Art Explorers was Book Bonanza. For three whole weeks they learned about all different kinds of book art. Leslie taught them how to make their own books from scratch. They used cereal boxes, cloth, butcher paper, scissors, and glue. They had to cut the cereal boxes and cover them in cloth, then fold the butcher paper accordion-style. They used a bone folder to make nice crisp creases, and they made paper hinges to hold multiple accordion sections together. When they were finished, you could really write in them. It took them two whole afternoons.

On the third and final Thursday of the session, Leslie showed them how, if they ran out of room in their books, they could add more pages by folding new lengths of paper accordion-style, and pasting these inserts onto existing pages. Like expanding staircases, they could be unfolded to extend up or down.

"You could just make a new book," said Carla.

"You could," said Leslie. "But I wanted to keep using this one." And then she brought out her own homemade book, so swollen with extra pages, it had to be held together with a ribbon around its middle. When she untied the ribbon, the book spronged open like a jack-in-the-box. She held it up and leafed through it slowly, unfolding its staircases as she went, so they could appreciate all its signs and wonders. Page after page she'd filled with her wild, loopy calligraphy, miniature portraits in oil pastel, fortunes from fortune cookies, tags from tea bags, candy wrappers from other parts of the world.

"That's sick," Carla said with approval.

"I'm doing that to mine," whispered Renu.

But Annamae—although she spent the rest of the afternoon like the others, pasting into her book paper stair inserts and also scraps from the cigar box where Leslie collected stuff for collages—knew that her real project would begin only later, after she got home. She would apply what she'd learned to Coco: paste vertical additions into the pages she'd already filled, so that she could go on using the little leather-bound book forever. It really could be forever. Because if you could add stairs to pages, couldn't you also add stairs to stairs? Build them up and up and down and down, extend them without end.

Around her, the other kids chattered busily.

"Oh, can I use that?" said Renu, already snatching the heart-shaped doily from the cigar box.

"Check out my manicure," said Carla, displaying the googly eyes she'd found in the box and glued to her fingernails.

The Art Explorers studio was a little room below street level. This afternoon, there were six explorers, Annamae, Renu, and Carla and three other kids. They sat on stools at high tables facing the windows, which were covered with wrought-iron grilles. Through them you could see people's feet, the occasional wheelchair or stroller, sometimes dogs. Leslie put on music while they worked and the day outside grew sootily dark and then turned streetlamp pink.

Dry leaves and pieces of litter whisked along the sidewalk. Annamae was not working. She was doing that thing she did when she thought, pulling out her bottom lip with her finger and thumb, but she was not even really thinking. She was simply with the leaves and plastic bags and Styrofoam blowing outside.

"Whatcha doing, Miss Annamae?" It was interesting. When they stopped calling Leslie "Miss," it was a sign of affection, and yet whenever Leslie called any of *them* "Miss," it was just the same.

Annamae turned to her dumbly.

"Building castles in Spain?" asked Leslie.

Annamae looked down. What castles? There was only the paper she had creased into accordion folds.

Leslie leaned over then and, just as if it were the most natural thing in the world, walked her pointer and middle finger slowly up the paper stairs, tread by tread.

Annamae's heart was like a paper bag someone had just blown into.

Before class ended, she found in the cigar box a mirror no bigger than a stick of gum. When no one was looking, she slipped it in her pocket. She would glue it on the cover of Coco.

Knife

"What are you doing?" Annamae's mother sounded horrified.

"Art."

"No. No. Absolutely not. Put the knife down." Her mother's face was pink from the shower and she wore only a towel. She had just happened to catch sight of Annamae on her way from the bathroom. "What are you *doing?*" she repeated.

Annamae had been trying to cut into the pages of a book with a paring knife. It was much harder than she'd expected. But she had taken proper precaution. "I'm using a cutting board," she pointed out.

"Yeah, you've got"—pause for a dramatic exhale—"you've got the blade facing your stomach. Anna*mae*." Her mother's shoulders, still wet, gleamed.

Annamae, twisting her bottom lip between finger and thumb, said nothing.

Then, with fresh annoyance: "What book is that?"

"Just an old one." Annamae held it up: a collection of fairy tales no one had looked at in a million years.

"But why cut it up?"

"Leslie showed us."

It was amazing, the images Leslie had shared with them during Book Bonanza. While the kids worked on making their own books from scratch, the teacher had pulled up on her phone examples of the opposite: art that started with already-made books and turned them into sculpture. Some of them you could barely tell had started out as books, that was how transformed they were. Some had been cut so that things—wagons, forests, ships—rose up out of the pages. Others had been cut so that things—ladders, honeycombs, tunnels—led down into the depths. One artist had even carved a book to look like rows of bookshelves that led farther and farther into the shadowy recesses of a library that seemed to go on without end.

"But she didn't tell you that you could do it yourself?"

"No."

"Well, you can't. I'm sorry. I don't want you doing this. That book I guess you can cut with scissors if you want—although you should have checked with me first—but you cannot use a knife." Annamae's mother took the knife, put it in the sink, and went to get dressed.

Annamae, with a crumpled feeling, bent to examine her handiwork. It was pathetic. She'd barely managed to make an inch-long gash go through a single page.

Paring

The same knife her mother had scolded her for using on the book was the one she was now being allowed to use for apples.

They had gone apple picking that morning with Rav Harriett and now they were all sitting at the wooden picnic table, working on an apple pie. Even Danny. Actually, Danny was more at the moment playing with the sugar bowl. Their mother was sifting flour, and Rav Harriett and Annamae were paring apples.

"Look how much you're wasting." Danny picked up one of Annamae's parings and showed her how much fruit she'd cut away along with the peel.

"At least I'm contributing."

"Give me your knife, then."

"Uh-uh."

He stuck the chunk of peel in the sugar bowl, then stuffed it in his mouth.

"Mom. Did you see what he just did?"

"Hmm? No. What did he do?"

Rav Harriett swiftly interjected, "He dipped a bit of apple in sugar, which is similar to the custom on Rosh Hashanah of dipping apple in honey. To symbolize a sweet new year."

"Do we have honey, Mom?"

Their mother brushed her floury hands on her apron and got the honey bear from the cupboard.

"It's because you're here, she's letting us," Annamae informed Rav Harriett.

All four took a piece of apple and squeezed some honey on top. "*Shanah tovah u'metuka,*" said Rav Harriett. "Happy new year."

"Happy new year! Wait, Danny," said Annamae, "toast." They touched their apple pieces together like wineglasses.

"There's another tradition with honey, when children first go to school," said Rav Harriett. "They would spread a little honey on the letters of the *alef-bet* and let the children lick it off. The idea was to let them know that learning is sweet."

In a flash, Annamae had hopped off the bench and started plucking pieces of the magnetic alphabet off the fridge.

"No," said her mother.

"Why not?"

"Sweetie, because. Gross. We're not going to lick honey off those. Put them back."

Sulkily, Annamae stuck the plastic pieces back on the door.

"But I know another custom," their mother said, "that has to do with letters and apples."

"What's that, Jo?"

"You take a peel"—she selected one of Rav Harriett's parings, which had come out longer and leaner than Annamae's—"and toss it over your shoulder."

"Say what?" Danny exclaimed as their mother threw food.

"Then you look at the shape it makes, and that's the first initial of the person you're going to marry."

"For real?"

"That doesn't look like any letter."

"It does kind of look like a *J*."

"More a lowercase *r*."

"That's because you're looking at it upside down."

"I want to try."

They all took multiple turns until the floor was strewn with apple peel.

"Look, it's an O," said Danny.

"Look, it's a mess," said their mother.

"Look," said Annamae, with a special smile for Rav Harriett. "It's signs and wonders."

Tea Party Game

Uncle Hersh and Aunt Marni had two children, too, also a boy and a girl. Shayna was three years older than Annamae and Gershom was seven years older. On the Fourth of July, they always went to Uncle Hersh's house, which had a pool. Last year Shayna had taught Annamae how to play underwater tea party. You sat cross-legged on the bottom of the pool and the host poured "tea" in your "cup" and you had to stir it with your "spoon" and drink it before rising back up to the surface. It didn't work for Annamae. She kept bobbing up before finishing her tea.

"You're too light," said Shayna.

This year, Annamae asked Shayna if she wanted to play, but Shayna said, "No thanks." She wanted to lie on the float and work on her tan.

Shayna was already the color of a perfectly toasted marshmallow. She wore the thinnest gold chain around her wrist and the thinnest gold chain around her neck. Her dark straight hair gleamed like a vinyl record. She had started shaving her legs.

Gershom didn't go in the pool. He lay on a chaise lounge with a book and wouldn't take off his shirt, not even when Aunt Marni said, "At least take off your shirt. I'm hot just looking at you."

Danny wouldn't play tea party, either. "I can't," he said. He was working on his dive. Nana was coaching him. He was very intent. He kept diving in, getting out, and returning to stand, dripping, again at the side of the pool. "Toes over the edge," Nana would say. "Tuck that chin." Each time he did a belly flop, Nana said, "Oof!"

More people arrived and the grown-ups went through the house to greet them. Annamae could never keep straight who they were related to and who were just friends. "You shouldn't say 'just friends,'" said Danny. He was sitting on a chaise lounge now, wrapped in a towel, his eyes all red and puffy from chlorine.

They began to have the conversation they always had when they got together, about how, exactly, they were related.

Shayna always started it. "What is it again? Our father is your mother's cousin . . ."

"So that makes us second cousins," said Danny.

"I thought we were once removed."

"Removed is for a different generation," Gershom explained, closing his book over one finger. "We're the same generation as Danny and Annamae."

"So we're first cousins?"

"No, look. Grandpa is Nana's brother, okay?"

"I know, I know—wait. So Grandpa's their third cousin!"

"No!" shouted Danny and Gershom together, cracking up.

Shayna gave a shriek and slapped at the water to splash them, but she was laughing, too.

It was always this way. At the beginning they were cool and stiff with one another, but they warmed up by the end, only after they'd been left to themselves, without any grown-ups, for a while.

Later, Annamae was sitting at the edge of the pool, a towel around her shoulders, when Uncle Hersh came out to start the grill. The boys had gone inside. Shayna rolled off the float, swam to the end of the pool, and lifted herself out. Her hair was slick and gleaming black.

Uncle Hersh stood beaming at her, his drink held low at his side, as if he'd forgotten it was there. He also had a gold chain, a thicker one, around his neck.

"What?" said Shayna, wringing out the end of her hair.

"I was just thinking," said her father. Annamae felt almost sorry for him, the way he was grinning so helplessly, with so many teeth.

"What?" said Shayna again.

Uncle Hersh moved his wrist and the ice cubes clinked. His smile was like the front part of an expensive car. "I created you."

Later, when they were driving home, Annamae leaned forward from the backseat and told her mother what Uncle Hersh had said. She was surprised and delighted when her mother made a farting sound with her mouth.

Unknown

Another time at Uncle Hersh's it was Annamae who didn't care to go in the pool. Danny was spending the weekend at Dante's. Gershom was doing something called "test prep." Shayna had a friend over and they'd gone inside to make a snack. They'd invited Annamae to go with them, but only after Aunt Marni called Shayna back and spoke to her in a low voice, so when she did ask, Annamae had said, "That's okay, thanks." Now, the only kid at the pool, she was sitting on her towel, reading a book.

Her mother and Nana and Aunt Marni chatted on chaise lounges behind her. Uncle Hersh was in the water alone, swimming slow laps. He was very tan. He finished his laps and swam over to the side of the pool by Annamae.

"Annamae."

She looked up politely.

"Annamae. Don't you want to come in?"

"No, thank you."

"Why not?"

"It's too chilly for me."

"You didn't even try it."

"I did." She said it very politely.

"No you didn't."

"I did!" She gave a little laugh that grown-ups liked. "I felt it with my hand."

"I didn't see you."

She gave one more polite smile and went back to her book.

"Annamae. Let me see you try it. The water's beautiful. It's warmed up since you tried it."

"If you didn't see me try it, how do you know it's warmed up since then?" Sometimes what grown-ups liked was not for you to be completely meek and polite, but to act a little smart-alecky. Within limits.

Uncle Hersh didn't let up. "I promise," he said. "It's perfect." He was resting his elbows on the lip of the pool and you could see the length of his body bobbing lazily out behind him. "Come on, Annamae. How often do you get to be by a pool?"

She gave another little laugh, hating how it sounded.

"Annamae, would you come here, please." This was her mother, speaking sharply. "I want to put some more sunscreen on your back."

Annamae went, biting a smile off her lips. It wasn't from happiness at being rescued. It was more a surplus of discomfort leaking out of her mouth.

On the way home, in the middle of silence, she burst out, "No one can tell another person the water's perfect, because how do they know what's perfect for you?"

"I feel you," said her mother. Danny had taught her to say that, instead of "I hear you," which he said made her sound like a hippie.

"Not even you," continued Annamae, with some passion. "Even if I trust you, even if you really, really try, you can never know exactly how I feel."

"True dat," said her mother. Danny had taught her to say that, instead of "You're right," which he said made her sound like a know-it-all.

There was something more to be said here. Annamae groped around for what it was. She'd started out full of a righteous need to make a point, but what came next was not so much a cry of vindication as of dismay. "No two people can ever know the exact same thing!"

Idea Game

They were having trouble coming up with ideas.

They were midway through fourth grade now, and Leslie had designed a new session of Art Explorers just for them. It was called Terrific Tricksters. Week one, she read them stories about Anansi and Coyote and Sun Wukong, the Monkey King. They looked at examples of traditional Ashanti and Miwok and Chinese drawings, and then the kids made illustrations for each of the stories in imitation of the different styles of artwork. That was not the problem.

The problem came in week two, when Leslie announced it was their turn. The kids were supposed to come up with their own trickster figures, and choose any medium they wanted to make them. By now they knew what *medium* meant, and they were well acquainted with the studio's supplies: paint, FIMO, Popsicle sticks and yarn, tissue paper and Mod Podge, colored sand, calligraphy pens, fabric, needles, thread, whatever. They loved it whenever Leslie gave them carte blanche, which was the Art Explorers way of saying free choice. This was not the problem, either.

In fact, they were eager to begin.

"I'ma do the Monkey King," announced Carla right away.

"That's been done," said Leslie. "You need to come up with your own idea."

"How about a leprechaun?" suggested a boy named Edson.

"Your own idea," Leslie repeated. "From your *heeaaad.*" She tapped her yellow-and-black head wrap.

"It has to be something that doesn't exist?" asked Renu.

Annamae laughed. "Leprechauns don't exist."

Renu made a dainty, annoyed sound with her tongue. "I mean it has to not even exist in pretend?"

"Well," said Leslie. "I'm not the art police. But inventing your own thing is part of the fun. Isn't it?" She looked at each of them in turn. "You get to make up any kind of creature you want. What's your trickster going to look like? What kind of things does it do?"

They were stumped.

"Really?" said Leslie. "Usually you guys are full of ideas."

Not today.

"Okay. That's okay. That happens. You know what? This is good; this is part of being an artist. I'm going to show you a cool way to get ideas. Everybody, get off your stools. Come on. Come down on the floor."

"That's where the ideas are at?" said Carla.

"Come on, Miss Carla. Everybody, come on. Come sit."

They all climbed down and sat on the floor. Leslie turned off the lights and sat with them. From down here, the studio felt like a cave. The only light came in through the two high windows with their wrought-iron grilles that looked out on passing feet. For some reason they had all gotten really quiet, like they were hiding. A little sloppy-haired dog came over to the window. It seemed to be peering in at them. The kids giggled, then hushed themselves.

Leslie said, "I invite you to close your eyes."

Annamae did. Right away she felt different. The giggles left her stomach. She felt herself grow hollow and expand. Everyone else must have felt it, too, because no one was making a sound.

"Let yourself take a deep breath," said Leslie. "Fill your lungs. Feel the air travel through your whole body."

Annamae felt it swirl through the hollow space inside and carry her out beyond her skin. It was almost frightening. As if she was not herself only but also part of something else she could never name.

"Now," came Leslie's voice again, "I'm going to offer you two good ways to receive an idea. One is to visualize it rising up through water."

Annamae found herself visualizing Shayna's tea party game. Trying to remain on the bottom long enough to drink her pretend tea. Here in this underwater cave, all quiet and liquid and cool. Light played across her eyelids, same as the light that wavered beneath the surface of the pool.

"The other," said Leslie's voice, "is to visualize it floating down from above. Go ahead and turn your hands palms up on your knees."

Annamae did.

"See if you can feel it float . . . right . . . down . . . into . . . your hands."

But it was she who seemed to be floating. She who seemed to be no more than an idea, adrift.

Belief

"How'd it go?" Leslie wanted to know once they'd all opened their eyes.

Hands shot into the air. Renu said she got an idea for a trickster in the form of a girl who was only a couple inches tall and would hide in her desk at school and give her all the right answers when she had to take a quiz. Carla said she got an idea for a trickster in the form of a talking wolf who gave bad guys the wrong directions on the subway. Edson said he got an idea for a trickster in the form of a giant forklift that could lift people's buildings when they were asleep and set them down in a different country, so they would wake up near their fathers.

A flurry of overlapping voices. Cupboard doors banging open and shut. Stools scraping across the floor. "Leslie, Leslie, where's the thingies you put in the glue gun?" "Can I get some of those pipe cleaners?" "Can we use the stuff in the cigar box?" The overhead lights snapped back on. Annamae remained on the floor.

"What's up, Miss Annamae?" Leslie put a hand on her shoulder.

"I didn't get any."

"Any what? You need some supplies?"

"Ideas."

"Oh. The visualization didn't do it for you?"

Annamae shook her head.

"You know you have to believe for it work. You must not have believed enough."

"I did," Annamae replied in a small, tight voice.

"Never mind," said Leslie. "I'm just playing." She gave Annamae's shoulder a little rub. "The only thing you really have to believe in is yourself."

In the end, Annamae wound up using the Fairy Man/ Ferryman. That's what she called her trickster. She didn't use any special supplies, just charcoal and a piece of cardboard. She drew him just as he was: a big bulky man with dark curly hair and a dark curly beard and a boat. And wings.

"Cool, cool," said Leslie, looking over her shoulder. "What makes him a trickster?"

What made him a trickster was that he ferried things not only from shore to shore but from world to world.

"Like intergalactic? Like from Earth to another planet?" asked Carla.

"Or you mean from real life to pretend?" asked Renu.

"It's all real," said Annamae.

She pretended not to notice Renu and Carla exchanging looks.

Nor did she tell Leslie that she'd cheated: She hadn't made the ferryman up.

That night after supper, Annamae asked her mother, "Do you believe in yourself?"

Her mother looked over the top of her readers. They were sitting in the living room part of the downstairs. Annamae was practicing dégagé, using the radiator as a barre. Her mother had been reading some student's dissertation chapters, making notes on them with blue pencil. "In what sense do you mean?"

Annamae shrugged. "I don't know. Leslie was saying today the most important thing is to believe in yourself." Now she switched to frappé, which meant striking the floor like a match. "Which is pretty funny, because we were also talking about believing in leprechauns and stuff."

"A whole different order of business."

"Yeah. Why do you need to believe in yourself? You know you're real."

"You know," her mother said musingly, and she paused to take off her readers. "The word *belief,* if I'm not mistaken, is linked to love. Etymologically speaking. The *lief* part—I'm pretty sure this is true—comes from a Proto-Indo-European root meaning 'to love.'"

Once again, Annamae was bowled over. Sometimes her mother's endless trove of linguistics facts could be annoying. Other times it made her think of a whole enormous ring of shiny metal keys, each with the power to unlock a tiny door. Like that whole wall of tiny doors at the main branch of the post office. Whenever her mother said something like this, it was as if she'd fitted her key into one and pulled it open, and for a few seconds you could peek through—and see that the other side was a wide-open space, vast as night, where everything met up.

"In that sense of the word," her mother said, reflecting, "I'd agree that belief in oneself is essential." She slipped her readers back on and returned her gaze to the manuscript in her lap. Her gaze, but apparently not her attention. Because a moment later she lifted her head again to add, "Essential, but not sufficient."

Annamae, who had moved on to practicing grand battement, grinned. She loved it when her mother argued with herself.

"As long as it's understood as a starting point," her mother went on. "Not the destination."

Two Hands Drawing

One afternoon shortly after she turned ten, Annamae was the sole Art Explorer. Renu was traveling to Pittsburgh to visit her aunt and uncle, Carla had gone to get a cavity filled, and the other kids signed up for that session were, for some reason, absent, too. So Annamae wound up having Leslie all to herself.

It was the third week of a session called Math Muse. The first week they'd made Möbius strips and then cut them in such a way that they fell apart into interlocked circles. The second week they'd made bilateral-symmetry and radial-symmetry drawings. This week was tessellations.

Being the only kid there put Annamae in a weird mood. It meant having the spotlight to herself: a chance to show Leslie how clever she was, especially now that she'd reached double digits. The way she'd do this was every time Leslie said anything, Annamae would respond by asking if that's what she really wanted. One of the older girls at school had been doing this the other day to the new young gym teacher, asking so innocently, he didn't catch on at first. When finally he said, "All right, sassy. Drop and give me fifty," he was joking, and the girl and all her friends fell out laughing, and the new young gym teacher had let out a chuckle, too. Annamae was eager to give it a try.

Leslie: "Draw a line in any shape you want—it doesn't have to be straight; it can be a squiggle, whatever—across the card, going from one side to the other."

Annamae: "Do you really want me to?"

Leslie: "Yeah. Go ahead."

Annamae smiled with her tongue pressed hard against her cheek.

Leslie: "Now draw another random line going from the top to the bottom."

Annamae: "You sure that's what you want me to do?"

This time, Leslie must have thought Annamae was confused, because she demonstrated. "Like this."

Each subsequent instruction—"Okay, take your scissors and cut the quadrants apart"; "Now rearrange them like this and tape them back together"—Annamae met with some version of "Is that really what you want?" and each time the bottled-fizz feeling increased inside her as she anticipated the moment when Leslie would catch on and crack up like the new young gym teacher had done, impressed with how witty she was. Finally, Leslie went over to the speaker and said, "We need some tunes. Elizabeth Cotten or Bessie Smith?" and Annamae responded, "Do you really want to know?" and Leslie said mildly, "I see somebody's being a wiseacre today," and Annamae exploded with laughter. But her face was very hot. It wasn't the lovely feeling she'd been expecting.

For the rest of the afternoon, Annamae didn't ask Leslie if she really meant what she said. She mostly didn't talk at all. Just followed instructions and traced the shape she'd made over and over on a large piece of drawing paper. They nestled into each other perfectly. Annamae didn't so much take pleasure in her own neatness as she did in the fact that the shapes behaved this way at all. She glimpsed the wonder of it, the way in which the phenomenon existed independent of her. Like a math thing. Like seven times thirteen. *She* didn't make it equal to ninety-one. It just was.

Leslie didn't say much the rest of that afternoon, either. After a while she pulled up a stool beside Annamae's and traced her own tessellations on a separate piece of paper.

At one point she unwrapped a butterscotch candy and put it in her mouth and offered one to Annamae, and they worked side by side then in silence, the only dialogue being the click of hard candy against teeth. And Elizabeth Cotten going, "Thought I heard a whistle blow / honeybabe Lord / Thought I heard a whistle blow." It seemed to Annamae that Leslie knew she was a little ashamed of how she'd acted, which was both a comfort and a confirmation of her shame.

When she had filled her whole sheet of paper, Annamae began to color in the shapes. She used a mixture of oil pastels and colored pencils, and as she went along she was amazed by how different the personality of each unit was—even though it was the exact same size and shape as all the others!—just by virtue of the way she colored it and its placement on the page.

Coloring, the thought came to her: If Carla had been the one acting like a wiseacre, it would have been completely different. Carla could have done the exact same thing and it would have been dumb and charming and no big deal. And yet in Annamae, the same behavior was a disappointment, ugly and irregular. She knew this was true, but she didn't know why. It made her feel lonely in the same way that Danny's saying, "Lighten up, Annamae" made her feel lonely.

Strangely, it also made her feel the opposite of lonely. The unlonely feeling of recognizing herself.

Annamae and Leslie both finished their drawings fifteen minutes before it was time for Annamae to get picked up. That was unusual—usually the kids were still working when their grown-ups came to get them—so what Leslie did then was also out of the ordinary. She went to the closet behind the desk and took out a big art book, and together they sat on the floppy couch by the entrance where the mothers and fathers and babysitters and nannies sometime waited when they were early.

There, with the book spread across both their laps, Leslie let Annamae be the one to turn the pages. The book was called *The Magic Mirror of M. C. Escher.* Some of the pages had just words, and some had math-type stuff, which was annoying in an art book, but some had drawings—tessellations, like what Annamae and Leslie had just made, only more complicated. There were flat geometric shapes that turned into ducks and fish. There were interlocking men on horseback, and winged cats. Some figures stepped through mirrors or crept up from the flat plane of the page. There were castles with impossible staircases, water that flowed up as well as down. There were ants and snakes and an eyeball with a dead person's skull reflected in the pupil. The pictures were grown-up in a way that seemed connected to Annamae's shame. Paging through them, she heard Danny's voice saying, "Lighten up, Escher."

There was one drawing that Annamae instantly loved. Or it wasn't that she loved it; it was that she recognized it. The instant she saw it, it made sense. She felt, oddly, that it belonged to her.

It was a hand in the process of drawing another hand, itself in the process of drawing the first hand.

"I know this picture," whispered Annamae.

"It's famous," Leslie told her.

But Annamae did not mean she had seen it before. She meant she knew it in her bones.

Search

In bed that night, she pasted a new paper staircase into Coco and on it she made a rough sketch of the Escher drawing. She knew she did a terrible job of it (hands were so hard to draw!), but she told herself it didn't matter, because it wasn't about trying to make something beautiful (as Ms. Jules would say); it was about reaching for something. About search.

Around the sketch (which wound up looking more like two ocean waves), she wrote in a circle (which took a long time; she had to keep turning the book around and around) these words:

I invent you
and you invent me
and I invent you
and you invent me . . .

And settling back against her pillow, looking over her drawing and her poem, her wish for what she wished for most, she was well content. She understood what she meant. Even if no one else on Earth ever would.

As soon as she arrived at that part of the thought—the possibility that no one else ever would—her contentment fled.

It was replaced not by sorrow, but by an awareness of what she lacked. And with it, a bright hunger—for the search.

Purses

As sixth grade began, some girls started wearing purses to school. Purses with unicorns on them, purses that were metallic, purses with leopard print, purses in the shape of a cat's head with ears sticking up. One girl had a purse that was like the diary Annamae had received for her sixth birthday: covered in pink fur. These weren't like knapsacks you kept in your locker; girls wore these all day long, on skinny straps that went across their torsos.

"You know what that means, don't you?" said Renu. They were sitting at a cafeteria table, Carla with her cardboard tray of school-bought lunch, Renu with her three-tiered round steel lunch box, Annamae with her boring old brown paper bag.

Carla and Annamae did not.

Renu leaned toward them, screening her mouth with her hand so they wouldn't have to see if there were any bits of food inside. "It means they have their period."

Annamae felt her mouthful of sandwich go dry, although she didn't know whether it was caused by the thought of girls getting their periods or by the excitement in Renu's voice.

"I got mine and I don't got a purse," scoffed Carla, sticking three ketchup-y fries in her mouth.

"You do? You did? When?" asked Renu.

Carla just looked at Renu, chewing.

"When?" pressed Renu.

"Earlier."

"Are you lying?"

Queenlike, Carla let her eyelids close.

Renu leaned in closer, her voice a razory whisper. "Have you had it at *school?*"

Carla opened her eyes. She inhaled, like when the doctor tells you to take a deep breath. Then, meaningfully, she exhaled.

"Oh. My. *God.*"

Annamae stood and carried her trash over to the bins underneath the basketball hoop. The cafeteria was also the gym.

All around her a fascination had been growing. Not only with purses and periods but also pop stars and pop songs, dieting and piercing, boyfriends and boy brows. Girls in her class called one another "bae" and "bruh." A new way of speaking had taken hold, with a new vocabulary everyone else had somehow instantly acquired. Annamae Galinsky, daughter of a linguist, alone had failed to become fluent. She saw herself standing on a beach as everyone around her ventured out to sea. Some on sailboats, some on motorboats, some on barges, some on blow-up rafts. One way or another, everyone else seemed to have found a way to ride the waves, while she remained planted, the sand dragging out from beneath her soles, and watched the others grow distant.

Instead of heading back to their lunch table, she pretended it took a long time to sort her compostables from her recyclables. The period was nearly over anyway. On the high-mounted clock, its face caged to protect it from errant basketballs, the long hand moved with a mechanical *ka-chunk.* She was getting lonelier by the minute.

Taxonomy

Sixth grade was when they started moving around for classes. For science she got Mr. T. His actual name, Mr. Tlaxcaltecatl, he wrote on the board the first day, then said, "But I know that's hard for you guys to say, so you can call me Mr. T.," and erased all the other letters.

When the bell rang at the end of the period and kids started filing out, Annamae, her heart hammering in her ears, went up to him. "I just wanted to say—did you know actually all babies are born being able to say all the sounds, in every language?"

He smiled at her. His teeth were as white as the inside of an apple. "Oh yeah?"

She nodded. The way babies learned language was actually by *losing* certain sounds. When her mother first explained this to her, Annamae had thought of the stories Rav Harriett told them. About how the world had been created out of the building blocks of the *alef-bet*. And how there was one missing letter. How only when the lost letter was restored would the world's brokenness be healed.

For just a second, it had made perfect sense. In order for a baby to learn language, it has to lose something it once had. She, Annamae, had once been able to produce all the click sounds, but in order to learn her mother's language, she had to lose that ability. In order for the *alef-bet* to build the world, it had to lose something, to lack something, to become a little broken.

But wait, what? In the next second, her understanding

dissolved like sugar stirred into hot tea. She was left only with the taste of having, for a moment, held the actual grains in her spoon.

Annamae felt herself getting sweaty, standing there before Mr. T.'s desk while students from the next class began to file in. She had to work to squeeze out the rest of what she wanted to say to him, now while the seventh graders were making noise behind her. "I know a lot of people don't really try. I mean, to say names right, from other languages."

Nobomi, whenever they went to a Starbucks, would always give her name as Naomi. When Annamae asked her how come, she said, "Some things are worth the fuss; some things are not."

Desks were scraping against the floor. Mr. T. was alternating between listening to her and greeting kids coming in the door. "But"—Annamae swallowed the excess saliva that had pooled in her mouth—"it doesn't mean we shouldn't try."

Mr. T.'s expression grew serious now. She could feel that he was mirroring her own. "That's very true," he said, nodding. "That's very true. I can tell you're a very thoughtful human being"—he glanced at the printed roster on his desk, traced his finger down the column of names—"Annamae Galinsky. Did I get that?"

She nodded.

"Yes!" He pumped his fist, flashed his apple whites, then said with a little bow, "I look forward to having you in class, Ms. Galinsky."

She left in a haze. Relief and elation swirled in her like glitter in a snow globe.

After that day, he never called her Ms. Galinsky again, and neither she nor any other student called him anything but Mr. T.

Annamae was telling Nobomi about this one

afternoon while they were sitting at the window table in Memuzin. Nobomi wasn't their babysitter anymore, Annamae and especially Danny being too old now for a babysitter, but sometimes she was their after-school companion. She had finished her coursework and most of her research and was writing her dissertation. It was called "Mother-in-Law Languages and Motherese: Avoidance Speech and Infant-Directed Speech in isiXhosa and Kambaata." Annamae loved hearing Nobomi recite the title. She would always ask, "What's the name of it, again?" and Nobomi would rattle it off like a piece of difficult music. Even after it became obvious it wasn't a real question, but a request, Nobomi would indulge her.

"Questions of curiosity," Mr. T. called real questions. As opposed to "questions of agenda."

Annamae told Nobomi about the distinction, how there were different orders of question.

"He sounds like a cool teacher," said Nobomi. "Your Mr. Taxonomy."

"That's not how you say it."

"How do you say it?"

"I don't remember," Annamae confessed.

Nobomi laughed at her.

"Stop!" she protested.

Nobomi reined the laugh in to a grin. Her teeth, too, were like the inside of an apple. Even more so because she was wearing fuchsia lipstick.

"You would make a cute couple."

Nobomi's eyes got big and round. "Is that sooo?" she said.

Annamae could feel her whole face burning. She changed the subject. "Can I get a halvah bomb?"

"You may. With two forks, if you please."

Annamae went to the counter and waited while Wasim made espresso for two men with mustaches like mice tails.

They drank them immediately, set their tiny glasses on the counter, and left.

"Yes, my friend?"

"Hey, Wasim. Can I please have a halvah bomb?"

He furrowed his brow and held her gaze, as if deliberating, before giving a single sharp nod and reaching into the pastry case for a slice of the chocolate tahini cake. It was an old routine. Pretending to consider her request before agreeing to it. He did it all the time.

"Oh!" said Annamae.

"You wanted something different?"

"No, no—that one's great, thanks."

It was just that she'd noticed how the joke worked. Wasim would pretend she asked a question of curiosity, when really he knew it was a question of agenda.

Necklace

It was a happy-sad day. Happy because today she was eleven, a number with bilateral symmetry, and because it was snowing and because—drumroll please, as Danny would say—Nobomi was taking her out for birthday lunch. Just the two of them.

Sad because it was also a good-bye lunch. Nobomi was moving to Baltimore for a postdoc, which made Annamae think of "What's up, doc?" which made her think of Bugs Bunny, which made it so the name Baltimore conjured carrots in her mind. She explained this to Nobomi over seitan club sandwiches.

"Cool brain." Nobomi stole one of Annamae's fries.

"I know." Annamae knew Nobomi would like this. She'd always been interested in Annamae's descriptions of the different colors and personalities of each letter of the alphabet. She was really the only person who'd ever let Annamae go on about it at length without getting bored. Sometimes she'd even venture her own associations. Always with a question mark, though, since Annamae was the expert. Nobomi would say, "I feel that *y* is magenta, with a rather wild spirit . . . a sort of a young rascally boy, is it?"

Annamae would take her time to consider before responding. "It *is*; it *can* be a very *dark* magenta, but it's more of an older woman. Kind of dignified but friendly."

Then Nobomi would gaze at her fondly and say, "Where oh where do you get these messages from? I would most truly like to know."

And Annamae would feel herself fill with grave happiness.

Now in the restaurant she tried to resurrect the old patter. "What does Baltimore make *you* think of?" She looked forward to visiting, and was eager for an association other than carrots.

Unexpectedly, Nobomi blushed. "Umm . . ." She gave a laugh, and looked off to the side. Out the window, small snowflakes were whisking and whirling about.

"What?" prompted Annamae.

Nobomi said shyly, "Baltimore makes me think of Marcus."

"What's that?"

"A man. My friend. Who lives there." Her blush deepened.

"You have avocado here." Annamae touched her own cheek to show where.

"Whoops." Nobomi used a napkin, then elongated her neck to present her face, glowing and beautiful. "Did I get it?"

Annamae nodded coldly.

When their plates had been cleared and they were waiting for their pieces of cake (but Annamae didn't feel like cake anymore), Nobomi slid a little box across the table. "Happy birthday."

Inside the box, on a bed of cotton, lay a tiny bottle on a silver chain. Inside the bottle, which was stoppered with an infinitesimal cork, Annamae could see a bit of paper rolled up and tied with the thinnest piece of string.

"Is it real?"

"What do you mean? It's a real necklace. Here, let me put it on for you."

Annamae came around the table and held her hair out of the way while Nobomi fastened the clasp.

"Do you know why it made me think of you?"

"Because you always say I get messages." Annamae turned back to face Nobomi. She held the bottle out from her chest and looked at it. It was barely bigger than a jelly bean. "Is there really something written on the paper?"

"I should think so. But don't try to open the bottle, or it'll break."

"What does it say?"

Nobomi had put on fresh lip balm after the sandwiches. Her smile glinted like mica. "Don't ask me; I'm only the messenger."

Mystery

After Nobomi moved to Maryland, Annamae wore the message-in-a-bottle necklace every day. After a while she noticed the chain would turn her skin a little bit green when it got wet, so she stopped wearing it in the bath. And her mother wouldn't let her wear it while sleeping, so each night she took it off and placed it in the little drawer built into the base of the mirror on her dresser. Other than that, it was always around her neck. She often wondered what the message written on the tiny scroll inside the bottle was, but, mindful of Nobomi's warning, she didn't try to remove the stopper and take it out.

After Nobomi left, whenever Annamae and Danny needed an after-school companion, they had a rotating series of grad students. There was a Laura, a Bill, a Paz, and a Valeria. All of them were fine, but none of them was Nobomi. Then the semester ended and Laura, Bill, Paz, and Valeria all went off to do other things, and even though their mother's schedule became more flexible when classes ended, there were still times when she needed a companion for the kids and so—drumroll please—then they had Nana.

Nana would take the train in from across the river and often she'd spend the night, or even two nights in a row. She'd sleep on the foldout couch and take up the top of the toilet tank with her electric toothbrush and what she called her "ditty bag"—a flowered, plastic, zippered pouch full of pills and lotions. She wore cotton gloves to bed and a shower cap in the shower. She did the dishes the second you put them in the sink. She was less of a companion than an intrusion. She definitely asked questions of agenda more than questions of curiosity.

Upon noticing Annamae wearing leg warmers with jeans, she asked, "Aren't those for dance class?"

"Sometimes, but they can also just be part of your outfit."

"Isn't that funny? In my day, we wanted slim-looking ankles."

Or when both Danny and Annamae wanted to go over and listen to the steel-drum players on the other side of the park: "Can you really hear music? My ears just hear noise."

Or one day when Annamae was sitting sideways across the armchair, reading a book: "What's that in your mouth?"

"My necklace."

"Should you really be sucking on it?"

Annamae let it sort of drip back out. "Why not?"

"You could choke."

"Nana, how could I choke if I'm wearing it on a chain around my neck?"

"It could come loose. Don't laugh. I once knew a girl who was sucking the bristle of her hairbrush. One of those big black bristles. It had fallen out, and she just put it in her mouth and was playing with it and then it was gone."

"She swallowed it?"

"No, she was certain she hadn't swallowed it."

"What happened?"

"Well, it was a mystery. Then a week or so later, she developed an itchy sore on the side of her neck. It turned out to be the bristle, working its way out of her body. It had entered one of her salivary glands."

"That isn't true."

"It is."

"Anyway, I don't think it's going to happen with my necklace. This bottle's bigger than a bristle."

"But sweetheart." Nana peered closer. "Aren't you ruining what's inside?"

Annamae looked. Nana was right. Her habit of sucking on the message in the bottle had damaged the stopper. The tiny paper scroll had gotten wet.

Forgetfulness

Very much to their surprise, they managed to convince Nana to take them to lunch at the Ferryman. It was surprising because (a) Nana, as she herself was forever saying, was very frugal, and (b) as their own mother had always maintained, children didn't belong in a bar. But the kids kept pointing the place out to Nana whenever they walked by, being sure to call her attention to how clean and spiffy it was, with light shining in the new plate-glass windows onto the marble bar top and the black-and-white tiled floor, and Danny kept talking about how curious he was to know what a thirty-dollar burger tasted like, and one autumn Saturday when their mother was at the language lab and Danny didn't have basketball, Nana said, "Well, my goodness. You only live once," and she got her purse and the three of them walked down the block.

Annamae had been a little nervous that the workers would be scandalized at the sight of them, and maybe even tell them children weren't allowed, but the greeter smiled as if she was delighted to see them, and once they were seated and looking at menus, it turned out the Ferryman served milk shakes as well as beer.

"Everybody looks normal," Annamae said after swiveling around both ways in her seat, taking careful stock of all the customers.

"What did you expect?" asked Danny.

"I don't know. Like old men drinking out of paper bags."

"Why would someone in a bar be drinking out of a paper bag?"

"It's a thing, Danny. People do it."

"Not in *bars*." He landed on the last word with such gleeful mockery, it made Annamae have to kick him beneath the table.

"Ouch," said Nana.

"Sorry," said Annamae.

Their milk shakes came, and first they blew their straw wrappers at each other and then they tried blowing bubbles in their milk shakes, but they were too thick and the kids wound up spurting splotches of milk shake out onto the table.

"Behave, please," said Nana.

"Yeah, behave, please, Annamae," said Danny.

"What, you started it!" cried Annamae.

Then someone came in who didn't look normal. He was so big, big tall as well as big wide, that the room grew noticeably darker while he stood up front, blocking some of the sunlight.

"I know that person," said Annamae, twisted around in her seat.

"No you don't."

He had dark curly hair and a dark curly beard. He was wearing an apple green baseball jacket. The greeter greeted him, then waved him toward the bar.

"Yes I do."

"What's his name, then?" asked Danny.

"He's the ferryman."

The man sat on a bar stool, his back to them, so they could see the big red wings embroidered on the back of his baseball jacket.

"You mean the owner? But how can you tell?"

"Not the owner. The ferryman."

Danny gave Nana a look like *Don't worry, she's always saying loopy stuff.*

"Don't you remember?" Annamae felt a rising distress. "I used to write him letters."

"Sure, sure."

"Sometimes you helped."

"Whatever you say."

"Danny!" She didn't know which was worse: that he really didn't remember or that he was pretending not to remember. Either way, she felt betrayed.

People at neighboring tables looked over.

"Indoor voice," said Nana.

The ferryman was not among those who'd looked over, but now, accepting a paper bag from the person behind the bar, he got up from his stool and walked out. She followed him with her eyes until he disappeared from view. She felt an excited confusion, also a wobble of doubt. Had that really been him? Would she see him again? Was the ferryman even real, or just someone she'd invented? And how could she ever know for sure? What would be the test?

"Remind me," asked Danny, grinning broadly. "What does the ferryman do?"

"Take people to and fro."

"To and fro to where?"

"The other side."

Danny did a giant cough into his fist that was really a laugh.

"Stop," Nana told him.

Tears filled Annamae's eyes. She pressed her napkin to her face.

"Lighten up, Annamae," said Danny, but he sounded embarrassed. Then he kicked the bottom of her shoe lightly, meaning *I'm sorry,* and she forgave him.

Their food arrived. All three had ordered burgers, and

they came on shiny brioche rolls and were wonderfully fat and drippy and required all of their concentration.

"Nana," said Danny at length. When she looked up, he subtly did that thing of pointing to his own chin to show her where she had ketchup on hers. He did it nicely, not making fun of her or anything. Just helping her out.

And it fell on Annamae very hard, the realization that Danny was rapidly becoming fluent in the language of adult manners. He was growing mature. Somehow that betrayal, unintended and beyond his control, hurt worse than his teasing. It was a form of forgetfulness, a sign that soon she would be even more alone.

Babble

"So, Danny," said Uncle Hersh from the head of the table. Which was unlike him, to initiate conversation. Usually he just sat, listening or maybe not. It often seemed as if he hovered in another atmosphere, his mouth in a vague smile that might have been just the shape his lips made when they were closed over his protuberant teeth. From time to time he'd rock the cut-glass tumbler he held and the ice cubes would clink, and Annamae always thought of this, more than his actual voice, as how Uncle Hersh sounded.

It was Thanksgiving and they were at Uncle Hersh's along with lots of other people Annamae saw no more than once a year. She still wasn't entirely sure which ones were related to her and which were relatives on Aunt Marni's side and which were just friends of the family. There had been a children's table and a grown-ups' table, but now dinner was over and dessert was more or less over and various people had gone off to lie down or watch TV, or both, freeing up chairs at the grown-ups' table, and some of the kids had wandered over.

Danny had come seeking a third slice of the chocolate cream pie and Annamae had come seeking her mother's ear. She brushed her mother's hair away and made a tunnel with her hands so no one else would hear. "How much longer would you say until we go?" She was wearing a dusty-rose corduroy dress, which she liked, and a pair of too-small tights, which were horrible. "They're giving me a stomachache," she whispered. "It really hurts."

"Go to the bathroom and take them right off," her mother whispered back. Not the answer she'd been hoping for.

Uncle Hersh cleared his throat. "Daniel," he said.

Danny sat down with his latest piece of pie and gave Uncle Hersh his attention.

"Your mother tells me you're not planning on becoming a bar mitzvah."

Danny smiled gently. Annamae admired him for that. "Um, yeah." He put a pretty big forkful of pie in his mouth. Annamae admired him even more for that.

"Danny," said Uncle Hersh again.

Aunt Marni said, "Hersh, stop it."

"I want to ask him a question. Danny."

Danny turned to him. He was still chewing, but he put his eyebrows up, nicely. Not always, thought Annamae, but sometimes Danny could be amazing.

"Help me understand. Why-y"—Uncle Hersh stretched the word into two syllables—"wouldn't you want to become a bar mitzvah?"

Aunt Marni said, "Oh Hersh, cut it out."

"I'd like to know." Uncle Hersh spread his palms as if to say, Could anything be more reasonable?

"I'm not really religious," said Danny. He was so patient and calm. Annamae didn't know how he managed it. Her own hands were damp.

"*Nu?*" Uncle Hersh grinned like he was turning over the winning card. "What difference does that make?"

"Hersh. Leave him alone," snapped Aunt Marni. To Danny, she said, "Don't answer him," and rolled her eyes.

Danny finished his pie. Somebody put on the kettle for tea. Somebody went to investigate the thuds coming from the playroom. Uncle Hersh went back to being his regular unspeaking self for the rest of the evening.

On the way home, Annamae piped up from the backseat. "How is Uncle Hersh like an infant?"

"What do you mean?" asked her mother.

"It's a riddle."

"Oh. How?"

"Because you said *infant* means someone who doesn't speak."

"I did?"

"Yes! Mom. Ety-mo-logically."

"Oh. Heh. True. You have a mind like a steel trap." A moment went by. "Although technically it means someone not capable of speech."

"That would be nice," said Danny. "If Uncle Hersh wasn't capable of speaking."

Their mother took one hand off the steering wheel and scruffed her fingers through the curls at the back of his neck. "You handled it well."

They drove along in silence, mile after mile, Danny asleep now up front, Annamae resting her chin on the back of her mother's seat and looking through the windshield, thinking thoughts. She searched for her star, sent it messages in her head—*I'm here! It's me. Where are you?*—but it didn't answer tonight. Not until the bridge lights came into view did she speak out loud again. "It only works if you don't count babble."

"What does?" said her mother.

"Calling babies infants. Because they can speak. It's just in another language, called babble."

Nobomi had taught her about babble. This was the language babies talked. Not only human babies—Nobomi said baby songbirds babbled, too. And just as human babies could produce the sounds of every language until they learned their own, baby songbirds could produce the sounds of other species. But only when they were new to the world, only before learning to sing their own songs.

Which they did by forgetting some of what they once knew.

Maybe there was a time, Annamae thought—in the dark, in the car, going through the tunnel that always brought them home—a time way back in the beginning, before memory, before that letter of the *alef-bet* went missing, when we really could all know the exact same things.

"Don't you think?" she asked groggily, not entirely sure whether she'd been babbling out loud or only in her head.

Her mother reached back and gave Annamae's bare ankle a squeeze.

In the end, Annamae had done as her mother advised: taken off her tights in the bathroom at Uncle Hersh's house. She'd stuffed them in the wastepaper basket. Her legs were cool and free.

Measuring

That December, she turned twelve. She was the last kid in her grade to turn twelve.

"This is the worst year of my life," she told her mother.

"Lighten up, Annamae," counseled Danny from the kitchen.

"I wasn't talking to you!" she shouted. "You're such a . . . a . . ." She cast about, but nothing good came to mind. "Doof!"

She could hear him snicker.

Annamae was lying the wrong way around on her mother's bed, which she still thought of as a queen bed, even though now she was old enough to know it was actually called a queen-*size* bed. Her mother was lying the right way around, propped against the headboard. They both had colds just bad enough to grant themselves a lazy Sunday. Her mother was working on the acrostic and Annamae had been trying to read a book she'd pulled randomly off her mother's shelf. The first page had seemed easy enough—something about a man who'd lost his umbrella—but it quickly grew strange and then impossible. Not the words, but the way they were put together. Which was a puzzle unto itself: How was it you could understand all the words but not what they were saying?

Annamae had long been in the habit of taking books from her mother's shelves in order to test herself against them. It was a way of measuring how she was coming along. Like how her mother measured her and Danny's height every year on their birthdays, making a mark on the doorjamb of the pantry. She'd take a book, read a page, and see if it came to life. To date, it never had. The blocks of text remained impenetrable. It was like pushing against a wall, looking for the spring that would open a hidden panel. So far, not one budge.

Still, she held to the belief that one day she would be able to step through.

"Why is it the worst year?" asked her mother.

"Because—" began Annamae.

Her mother blew her nose like somebody in a cartoon.

"Be-*cause*"—superpatiently, Annamae began again—"I don't have any friends. Renu's gone. Carla doesn't like me. I'm ugly. I can't even read." She let the book slide to the floor with a thunk.

"Annamae. Please don't wreck my books."

Renu's family had moved back to Pittsburgh in November. Carla had been moved into all classes for kids who needed extra help. And Annamae's nose had recently gotten bigger than the rest of her face. It was definite. She'd been tracking it each night before going to sleep, studying it in the little mirror glued to the cover of Coco. The mirror was so narrow, her whole nose didn't even fit in it anymore.

Her mother stroked Annamae's foot. "What about all those kids who were just here for your birthday?"

Four girls from school. For gifts, they had brought a babyish kit for making potholders, a magnetic dry-erase board for her locker, a microbead pillow that looked like a jelly doughnut, and a set of bath bombs that looked like macarons. For an activity, each girl had decorated her own gingerbread house. They finished too early and then mostly just sat around the wooden picnic table ("I can't believe this is your dining table!" one girl had exclaimed. "Did you, like, steal it from a park?"), gorging on the leftover decorations and debating the lyrics of songs Annamae didn't know.

"They're fine, I guess. They're just not my friends."

"Poor Anomenon."

Annamae looked up quickly to see if her mother was making fun of her, but her expression was soft. Her nose was red and her eyes looked teary.

"Are you crying?" Annamae was a little appalled.

Her mother shook her head. "It's just this rotten cold," she explained nasally, holding up a crumpled tissue for evidence.

"Yeah, and on top of everything I have a cold!"

"That clinches it," agreed her mother. "Being twelve really is the pits."

Failing

Mrs. Altschuler sent a report home. Annamae was on track to fail English.

"How could you be failing English?" asked Annamae's mother.

Annamae, lying on her own bed for once, let out a groan.

"I'm asking a question of curiosity," said Annamae's mother. She'd learned the parlance from Mr. T. at parent-teacher night. "I'm genuinely curious about how you, the daughter of a *linguist*"—the word came out of her mouth as if from a slingshot—"could manage to fail the subject of *English*."

That rhymes, thought Annamae. Actually, no, it didn't rhyme, but almost. It was a near rhyme, which was an actual thing she had learned about from her mother.

"Anomenon. Can you talk to me about what's going on?"

Annamae, curled on her side, eyes shut, shook her head.

Her mother breathed deliberately. *Breathing in, I know I am breathing in,* said the app her mother listened to when she meditated. *Breathing out, I know I am breathing out.* Danny did an impression where he managed to act out both their mother meditating on her little bamboo meditation bench and the man on the recording.

"Okay," her mother continued, when it became clear she was going to have to keep up both sides of this conversation on her own. "I kn— I believe you're not failing English because you're incapable of the work. So. I'm thinking it's about something else."

Annamae could feel it, her mother's thinking. She felt it as a kind of mental scribbling, an invisible pencil sketching geometries in the air.

"Is it a problem with the teacher?"

Vigorous head shaking. Annamae liked Mrs. Altschuler, which made not doing the work more painful. That was the reason she was failing: She wasn't doing the work. She hadn't handed in any of the assignments this entire quarter.

"So . . . you got an A first quarter, an A second quarter, and this quarter you're on your way to earning an F."

Annamae understood she was supposed to break the silence. She felt how powerful she was, not breaking it. It was exhilarating and terrible.

"Are you having a problem with any of the kids in your class?"

More head shaking.

A siren went by, avenues away.

"Are you sad, Annamae?"

She shook her head again, not vigorously. Then she opened her eyes, rolled onto her back, and qualified her answer. "I mean, sort of. But that's not why."

"Would you say more? I promise to just listen."

She wanted to say more. She wished it were possible.

Her mother chewed her lip and went to smooth some hair off Annamae's forehead, which sent Annamae promptly back into fetal position. She listened to her mother inhale deeply and exhale slowly. *Breathing in, I notice my thoughts. Breathing out, I let my thoughts go.*

Until, unable to let them go, her mother spoke again. "I'd really like to understand, honey."

Those were the saddest words. They made Annamae so, so sad.

Doomed

This was what Annamae had realized. No one could ever understand anybody. Not really.

They were all doomed.

Doomed not to understand one another.

Worse: doomed to go around thinking they *were* understanding one another, thinking they *were* being understood.

It was language's fault. People mistook language for solid ground, when really it was a just a net.

All people could ever do was try.

And fail.

Their words spilling like pennies through the holes.

Special

Anyway, Uncle Hersh had had it wrong. Danny was going on fourteen. If he'd been going to have a bar mitzvah, he would have had to start preparing more than a year ago.

It was the kids in Annamae's grade who were preparing for theirs. They talked about their themes. One boy was having a baseball-themed bar mitzvah, another had the theme of a pool party. A girl whose theme was candy said she was having her portrait done by an artist who worked exclusively in M&M's. Another girl's theme was making a hundred loaves of challah to donate to a soup kitchen.

"Can I have a bar mitzvah?" asked Annamae.

"No," said Danny.

"I wasn't talking to you, jerkwad."

"Annamae!" Their mother sounded legitimately shocked.

"Sorry."

They were having leftover lentil soup, leftover eggplant pizza, and leftover chicken thighs with olives. It was "clean out the fridge" night. Outside the kitchen window, snow was falling in a cone lit by the streetlamp.

"'Jerkwad,'" their mother repeated. "'Jerkwad.' What does that even mean?" Now she sounded more professionally interested.

"I don't know."

"'Jerkwad.'"

"Mom." This was Danny.

"What?"

"Stop. It's embarrassing when you say it."

"Mom." This was Annamae. "Can I? Have a bar mitzvah?"

"No," said Danny, sliding the last slice of pizza onto his plate. "Bar mitzvahs are for boys. You mean can you have a bat mitzvah."

"Fine, can I have a bat mitzvah?"

"Why do you want one?" asked their mother, reaching over to Danny's plate, cutting the last slice down the middle, and removing half onto her own plate.

"I just do."

She had been to Gershom's and she had been to Shayna's. Gershom's she didn't remember at all. Of Shayna's, all she remembered was there had been a dolphin sculpted out of ice. And she had tasted shrimp for the first time. And spit it out into a lavender paper napkin decorated with Shayna's name in purple.

But no, that was not all.

She remembered sitting in synagogue, with its heavy, ugly stained-glass windows, and the smell of furs, and the Mary Janes that pinched her feet but also pleased her with their shininess. She remembered the fake diamond glued to the toe of each shoe. And this one particular moment out of the long, boring ceremony, when someone—the rabbi?—had said, "Shayna is a very special girl," and Shayna had cried and Aunt Marni, standing up at the front of the synagogue with her, had cried, and Annamae had thought with awe and jealousy, Shayna is a very special girl.

Shayna, whose hair shone like the grooves in a record album.

Am I? she'd wondered with a sick sinking feeling. She'd looked down at her fake diamond toes. Will anyone ever say that about me?

Now in the kitchen with the snow falling outside the window and Danny laughing silently at her across the picnic table, she speared a leftover olive with her fork and repeated, "I just do."

Play

Annamae and her mother got called in, both of them together, for a conference with Mrs. Altschuler. They sat in the classroom with its bleach-smelling linoleum floor and its buzzing fluorescent lights and its poster that was supposed to make middle-school students think English was cool because it showed William Shakespeare wearing a pair of sunglasses over the caption *I invented swag,* and the space that was normally utterly ordinary to Annamae was made exotic by the absence of kids and the fact of her mother sitting in a chair with a hinged arm desk. She felt like they were in a play.

Mrs. Altschuler came around to sit in front of her desk, her back to the wall of windows. The windows were divided into an astonishing number of panes. Sixty, to be exact. Annamae had counted them many times. Outside each of the sixty panes, snow was coming down.

Annamae thought, Wouldn't it be funny if one of the sixty panes had no snow coming down? Like a rip in the scenery, letting you glimpse backstage. Letting you know this was just a play. All of a sudden she remembered a thing from when she was little, one time when she'd tried to ask her mother about a realer world beyond this one. This memory had something to do with a windowpane, too. A windowpane showing her reflection, and something else? Her reflection doubled. A vision of her but not-her on the other side of the glass.

Mrs. Altschuler opened the file folder that contained

the benchmarks and assignments for the third quarter, and then she opened the file folder that had Annamae's name printed on a little sticky label on the tab and showed how it held nothing but air. "Even if she were to hand in a little of the work, so I could give her partial credit?" the teacher was saying. With her old-timey accent, the word *little* got broken in two pieces, like a saltine. She didn't pronounce the *t* sound at all. Annamae envisioned it, the letter *t*, crumbled into cracker dust.

"What do you think about that?" asked her mother. "Annamae?"

"Sorry—what?"

Her mother sighed. *Breathing out, I release any tension.*

Mrs. Altschuler tapped her eraser on the form that listed the benchmarks. She moistened her coral lips, something she did about a hundred times a day. She had a way of doing it—her tongue poking straight out—that made it look like she was getting ready to blow a bubble. "Annamae. Mom has taken off work to be here today."

"I know." It actually wasn't true. Her mother didn't go to the language lab on Wednesdays. Pretending was easier than explaining, but it made her feel even more that they were actors in a play, speaking their lines, going through their artificial motions.

She studied the sixty windowpanes. If only one of them had blue sky instead of snow. Blue sky with little white butterflies. She'd point it out to her mother and Mrs. Altschuler: *See? There's a hole in the backdrop. There really is another world beyond this one.* They'd look and gasp and clutch their throats. *Oh Annamae, you were right. Now we understand what you've been trying to say all along. You really are a very special girl.*

"So," Mrs. Altschuler was saying. "We can all come up with a plan for you to get your work done. Agreed?"

What could Annamae do but drift away? Float out

of her body toward the windows with their dozens of panes, pass through them into the ether full of tinky little snowflakes swirling around like Escher animals eating one another's tails, soar beyond them into the seen and unseen city. Fly above the streets burdened with lumbering buses and trucks and cars. Notice everything. Phlegm spat on sidewalks, men in stilettos and long fur coats, halal stands, yellow-eyed fish on beds of ice, scraggly trees inside wrought-iron wickets, uniformed school girls with gold hoop earrings, figures sleeping on cardboard, old women wheeling their laundry and lapdogs in folding shopping carts.

It wasn't that she didn't love this world.

"Annamae."

"What?"

It was that she knew it wasn't everything.

Maybe Mrs. Altschuler had the same app as her mother. Now she seemed to be breathing mindfully, too.

"Sorry," said Annamae.

Perhaps she shouldn't have been born a person.

Bees

The problem was creative writing.

That was the curriculum for third quarter sixth-grade English. They started with Character Building Worksheets, where they were supposed to come up with names, ages, nationalities, genders—a whole list of Identifying Characteristics they had to select for their fictional characters. Then came Paragraphs of Detailed Description: Using Modifiers and Avoiding Cliches. Then Vignettes With Action: Events Unfolding in Time. Then Vignettes Involving Two Characters: Formatting Dialogue. And so on until the final project: a Short Story with Introduction, Rising Action, Climax, Falling Action, and Denouement.

Annamae wouldn't agree to do it. Not any of it.

"Is it that it feels too rigid? Too formulaic?" guessed her mother on the subway home.

But no, that wasn't it.

They went a whole other stop before her mother tried again. "What if we started backward—we could come up with the idea for a story first, then go back and I can help you break it down to complete the earlier steps?"

Annamae lifted one shoulder in a shrug.

"It seems like a pretty neat assignment." How careful her mother was being. How grindingly delicate. "But challenging also. To come up with a story."

A woman sitting directly across from Annamae was applying purple mascara with a tiny wand. Beside her slept an old man, one hand, turned upward on his thigh, trembling in a manner apart from the vibration of the train. Beside him, another man, wearing lime green headphones, looked up from his phone, saw Annamae watching him, gave her a businesslike nod, and went back to the screen.

There was no shortage of stories.

"Everybody loves this unit," Mrs. Altschuler had said back in the classroom. "Most of the students, it's their favorite."

"I know it can be overwhelming once you fall behind," Annamae's mother said now. "I remember in college, oh man, when I had to take stati—"

"It isn't that."

"Could you try to tell me what it is?"

Annamae's only concession was to lean her head against her mother's shoulder. Her mother's beautiful gray wool coat. To thread her arm through her mother's. As the train threaded through the tunnels. Rocking.

That evening she listened to her mother on the phone with Nana.

When they first got home, Annamae complained her ear ached and her mother had let her climb into the big queen bed off the kitchen.

"Do I have a fever?" Annamae had asked while her mother frowned at the thermometer.

"I don't think this counts."

"What does it say?"

"Ninety-eight point nine."

"It really hurts. Do we have an onion?"

So now she lay on the sheets that smelled of apricot hand cream, a warm onion wrapped in one of her father's famous wool socks pressed not against her ear but against her neck, just behind the ear, where the heat felt lovely and the onion didn't prevent her from listening in on her mother's half of the conversation.

"She says she can't bring herself to make up a character she controls."

The snow had stopped. Across the street the office building was mostly dark—just a few lit windows here and there.

"I know," her mother was saying. "Not yet . . . The school social worker is supposed to be sending some names. . . . Yeah . . . yeah, Mom . . . I already left a message with the pediatrician."

As she watched, another cell lit up across the street. A figure came right over to the window and stood there, looking out. A lone bee.

In kindergarten they had taken a field trip to learn about honeybees. A lady in a white beekeeper suit, with a long gray braid hanging down over one shoulder, had pulled a frame out of a bee box so the kids could see the bees at work. They learned that when bees are happy, they give off a lemony smell, and when they're anxious, they give off a banana-y smell. They learned that bees live in colonies and share and cooperate. They learned that bees are always thinking not about themselves but about the whole hive. If a bee is sick, it won't even come back into the bee box, where it could infect the others. It just nobly goes off and dies.

"I don't think it's that," her mother was saying quietly on the phone. "It's something to do with not wanting to control the characters. Wanting them to be real."

The kids had all worn paper apples on pieces of yarn around their necks. Each apple had a kid's name printed on it, the name of the teacher and the school, and the phone number to call in case of emergency.

Annamae strained to hear, but her mother seemed to be just listening now.

They'd learned that bees communicate with one another. That bees tell one another where to find good flowers. Manny Gustav, who spent the most time sitting out recess of anyone in their class, started going, "Bzz bzz! Bzz bzz!" and other kids started to copy him. Their teacher said, "Everyone shush," and the bee lady said actual bee language isn't buzzing; it's dancing. And Annamae had wondered, If the bees' language is dancing, what is the bees' alphabet?

When next her mother spoke, she had dropped her voice even lower. But in their little apartment above the lighting shop, you could always hear everything. "She says—no . . . Mom, Mom, listen. She told me not even God would do such a thing."

Creation

Annamae didn't understand why it was so hard for people to understand.

Especially people who'd been there a long time ago when Rav Harriett told them the story of how the world came to be. How God had been playing, for delight's sake, with the signs and wonders (later to be known as the letters of the *alef-bet*), stacking them like blocks and tossing them in the air and spinning them like tops, turning them and turning them, and how from them—lo!—everything came to be.

Especially people who were linguists and took language seriously and who should understand that putting words together and inventing people and worlds and stories out of them should not be taken lightly.

Especially people who'd known her since she was born and therefore knew she'd loved—had a special relationship to and could even tell you the colors and personalities of!—the letters forever.

How could such people not understand that to use her power to put letters together to form words to form stories about imaginary characters who could never think for themselves, never do anything on their own, never meet her, see her, challenge or surprise her, who had no freedom or power of their own and could never keep her company—how could such people not understand that to invent such figures would hurt?

How could such people be surprised that Annamae Galinsky, serious to a fault ever since the crib, took the practice of creation seriously?

Solitary Bees

The bee colony thing turned out not to be true.

Or yes true, but only part of the story.

One sticky-hot night, Annamae and Danny had been flipping around the channels, struggling to agree on what to watch, when they'd come across a documentary on solitary bees. They both loved wildlife documentaries. They didn't even have to ask each other; it was obvious this was the show both would want.

They'd lain down on the floor, where it was slightly cooler, their heads propped against the couch, bowls of coffee ice cream propped on their stomachs, angling their bodies to catch the breeze from the box fan in the window, and together had learned that not only do some bees live alone but that of the thousands of bee species that exist, over 90 percent are solitary. Instead of congregating in hives, they make individual nests in the ground, or in tree stumps, or in crevices in walls, or in old abandoned snail shells.

These bees, the narrator said, spend their whole lives alone, from birth. When the mother bee is ready to lay an egg, she makes a little clump of pollen and nectar and puts it in a hole. That's called *provisioning*. Then she lays her egg on top of it and seals the hole with mud or leaves. When the egg hatches, the larva eats the ball of pollen and nectar. For eleven months it stays in the hole by itself, eating and growing into a bee. Then it comes out into the world and gets to work spreading pollen. "The solitary bee knows no loneliness," intoned the narrator.

"How does *he* know?" said Annamae.

"What?"

"That it knows no loneliness."

"Science," said Danny.

"Danny," said Annamae.

"Yeah?"

"This is when you're being so annoying."

Solitaire

Nana always kept a pack of playing cards in her purse.

"Why?" Annamae wanted to know. She'd been going through the purse, looking for a piece of gum. So far, no luck, but there were lots of other items of interest. A rain bonnet folded up inside a little plastic envelope, a package of tissues, keys, coins, bobby pins, a wallet, a nail file, dental floss, ticket stubs, safety pins, a pocket calendar that said *Georgette's Dry Cleaning* on the front, a cute little magnifying glass.

"I'm a card fiend," said Nana.

It was true they always played cards when they went to Nana's house. In addition to Liverpool, she'd taught them to play Scat, Gin, and Spoons. But even when she was at their apartment, if their mother was out and Danny and Annamae were busy doing other things, she'd take out her deck and play.

"Here, hand them over." Nana sat at the kitchen table and shuffled several times, making the bridge. Annamae loved that sound. Whenever she tried to do it, the cards went flying all over the place. Nana dealt the cards in a circle, twelve piles around the circumference and one in the middle.

"That's how you do it?" Annamae asked. "I thought you were supposed to lay them more in a row."

"That's Klondike," said Nana. "There're different versions. This is Clock."

It was boring but mesmerizing. Nana's hands moved

so quickly and she turned over cards with such a satisfying snap.

"In olden times, you'd play solitaire to find out who you were going to marry."

"What do you mean?"

"They used it for fortune-telling."

"How?" Annamae remembered the apple peels. "Tossing them over your shoulder?"

"I don't think so. I don't really know. It's just a fun fact. Maybe it had to do with the order of the cards as you dealt them."

"Do you believe in fortune-telling?"

Nana made a sound like *pfft*. "I don't even put much stock in the weather forecast."

"Belief means love."

"Does it?"

"Something like that."

Nana clucked her tongue and kept turning over cards and sliding them into piles. After a while, she said, "Heh! I think I'm going to win. And I didn't even cheat."

"Nana! Why would you cheat?"

"Poor moral fiber."

"Anyway, you play so much, it must be easy for you to win."

"Not this game, honey. This game's pure dumb luck."

Stellar

She went to the psychologist recommended by the school social worker. His name was Dr. Pekkar. "Almost like the soda," said Dr. Pekkar while shaking Annamae's hand.

"Oppositional defiant disorder," said Dr. Pekkar to Annamae's mother after the session while Annamae sat in the waiting room and played with the noise machine, switching it from Ocean to Rain to Brook to Thunder.

"Oppositional defiant disorder, my ass," said Annamae's mother before they'd even gotten to the elevator.

They did not go back to Dr. Pekkar.

She went to the psychotherapist recommended by the pediatrician. His name was Mr. Smart. "Not so smart if he's only a Mr.," remarked Annamae on their way to the appointment.

"Don't be elitist," said her mother. "An MSW could be a better therapist than an MD. Most MSWs are *probably* better therapists than MDs."

Mr. Smart rubbed his eyes a lot. He mentioned executive function disorder and said they should get a neuropsych eval.

"Eval, eval," said Annamae as they stood waiting for the elevator. "Not so smart if he can't even say the whole word."

"Annamae," said her mother.

She went to a neuropsychologist her mother knew through the language lab. Her name was Ginny. "You've gotten so big," Ginny said, shaking Annamae's hand. Apparently, Annamae had met her before.

"What did she say?" asked Annamae after her mother hung up the phone with Ginny a week later.

"She's mailing the full report."

"But what did she say now?" The phone call had lasted almost a half hour. The psych eval, which had turned out to be a fairly enjoyable battery of quizzes, puzzles, and games, had lasted the better part of two days.

Annamae's mother was leaning against the wall by the landline, looking through narrowed eyes at Annamae and stroking her imaginary mustache. "She said you have a stellar brain."

Annamae made a sound that could only be called a chortle.

Her mother sighed.

"You should be happy!"

"Should I?"

"Hel-*lo*. 'Stellar,'" said Annamae, pointing at herself with both index fingers.

Her mother smiled grimly.

Annamae still refused to do the work.

Sorry

They hadn't seen Rav Harriett in forever.

"Not for*ever*," protested their mother. "When did we—we went apple picking, remember? When was that, last fall?"

The kids insisted it had been longer than that. Danny said it must have been two years ago because he remembered bringing back a sack of apples for his soccer team and he hadn't played soccer in two years. Annamae said it had to have been three years ago because she hadn't taken judo in three years. Danny said, "What does judo have to do with apple picking?" and Annamae said she remembered practicing her *ukemi* in the orchard. Their mother said it couldn't have been two *or* three years. "It's been just a little over a year," she decided.

"But why haven't we seen her?" Annamae asked. "What happened?"

"Nothing happened," said their mother. "I guess we just fell into different rhythms."

"Like Nana."

"What? No. Not like Nana." Her mother sounded annoyed.

Nana had had a tiny stroke. She was all better now except for something called ataxia, which meant she talked a little funny and she walked a little funny. And her eyeballs kind of didn't hold still. It made Annamae not want to see her so much anymore.

They were setting the table for Rav Harriett. It was a

Sunday afternoon, so blustery out that the windowpanes rattled in their frames. Their mother had made borscht from scratch, and also a kind of seedy cracker she insisted on calling "health crackers" even though the kids begged her not to. They were actually pretty good, almost as good as real supermarket crackers.

Their mother had put on a necklace made of little felted balls, each a different brilliant color, all sparsely strung on a piece of black floss. It made Annamae nervous, the necklace, the homemade crackers, the fuss. She understood it was proportionate to the worry she was causing.

Inviting Rav Harriett over had been Danny's idea. Annamae knew this because it was basically impossible not to eavesdrop on people in their apartment. Just a few nights ago she'd been in bed, all washed and brushed and in pajamas, the string lights that climbed like ivy across her wall casting their cheerful glow, and just as she took her library book off her bedside table, from downstairs came the sound of her mother crying. Or not quite, but speaking in an upset, breaky voice. At first, Annamae thought she must be on the phone with Nana. Then she heard Danny say, "Why don't you ask Rav Harriett to talk with her?" and she knew her mother must have told him the thing she'd said about God.

And Annamae was sorry. Sorry to make her mother cry, sorry to disappoint Mrs. Altschuler, sorry to waste so much money going to therapists (another overheard conversation, this one between her mother and the health insurance company), sorry to make Danny (whom she could hear now being amazing with his grown-up kindness) have to be comforting their mother, sorry she'd never probably be eligible to be called a very special girl. She was so sorry about that last thing, it made her throat hurt. Still. She was sorry, but she was not wrong.

If only she could make Mrs. Altschuler and her mother understand.

Suddenly into her head slipped Ms. Jules, her old ballet teacher from a million years ago, saying, *No no no no. Don't just make shapes.* Saying—what had she said?—*Really reach!*

What Mrs. Altschuler wanted them to do was make shapes.

It had the same dirtiness as pretending dolls were real.

It had the same loneliness.

From her bed, Annamae heard the sound of her mother crying and the even worse sound of Danny telling her it would be okay. Misery clotted her throat.

If only she could explain it wasn't a matter of being stubborn.

If only she could explain it was no good making up characters and being in charge of what they did and what happened to them. To be like Uncle Hersh standing at the edge of the pool, smiling his proud smile, clinking his ice cubes, saying, "I created you."

Where was the question of curiosity in that?

Lack Game

So Rav Harriett was summoned. In the days leading up to her visit, Annamae had felt the burden of knowing she was the reason for the visit. But as soon as Rav Harriett actually arrived, the whole house seemed to lighten from her presence. Her curls had turned grayer since they'd last seen her, and although she still wore her low high heels, even Annamae stood taller than she did now. But her eyes were the eyes of an inquisitive bird, and she had a way of saying freely whatever came into her head, no matter if it was part of the conversation. And then there were her lovely, atrocious table manners: She blew on her spoon. She slurped. She reached freely and often into the salt cellar with her fingers. She got borscht and salt and bits of seedy cracker on the table, and then got whatever she spilled on the table on her sleeves. It was as if she had no shyness, no embarrassment.

The kids had to work not to catch each other's eye, and even so Annamae could feel Danny biting his lip to hold back laughter.

If he thought he'd managed to conceal his mirth, Rav Harriett disabused him. "I may be lacking in neatness," she said, wetting her napkin in a glass of seltzer and calmly rubbing at a spot of borscht on her sweater, "but at least I'm not lacking in lack!" And, giving up on the stain, she helped herself to another ladleful.

Danny, caught, colored and coughed. But Rav Harriett's ease seemed to free his tongue, too. He said, "That's a *good* thing?"

"You'd better believe it." She stuck her spoon into the communal bowl of sour cream. "Just think"—swirling the dollop of white into the purple—"without lack, without hunger, I'd never know the pleasure of eating."

"Hmm," said Danny.

"Without hunger for knowledge," Rav Harriett went on, "I'd never know the pleasure of learning."

"Without hunger for adventure, you'd never know the pleasure of trying something new," their mother chimed in.

They went around the table then, coming up with examples. It was a game invented by no one. It had no name and no rules. It had welled up like a spring from the ground. The kitchen seemed to grow spacious and at the same time to contract cozily around them. The overhead light burned bright as the shortest day of the year slunk to a close.

"Without loneliness," said Annamae, "you'd never know the pleasure of company."

Rav Harriett looked at her across the picnic table. She didn't smile. The frown she was giving Annamae was better than a smile.

"Hey," said the rabbi. "You guys ever hear the story of Adam and Eve?"

Lack

Obviously they'd heard the story of Adam and Eve.

"But do you know about the strange punishment of the snake?"

Annamae shot a look at Danny: *Do I?*

He responded in kind: *Search me.*

Even their mother looked perplexed.

So Rav Harriett told them:

For beguiling the woman, for persuading her to eat the apple, God punished the snake. The punishment was: "On your belly you shall crawl, and dust you shall eat all the days of your life."

The ancient sages scratched their heads when contemplating this part of the story. They tugged on their beards and looked around the table in the study house and asked one another, "If the snake is going to eat dust, it'll never go hungry. What kind of punishment is that?"

It was very strange, everyone agreed.

Until one of the ancient sages, Rabbi Simcha Bunim, figured it out. He said, "Aha! That is the punishment: The snake will never know lack.

"The snake, unfortunately, has all its needs provided for."

Wait. What?

"Wait. What?" said Danny.

No One

"Hang on!" cried their mother. She swung her legs around, got up from the bench, and sped into her bedroom just off the kitchen. They all turned to watch her through the open door. She crouched by a bookshelf, mumbling half to herself, half to them, "Hang on . . . Hang on . . ." until she called, "Got it!" and strode back, book in hand.

Annamae turned her head sideways to see what was on the cover. Just writing. *Parables and Paradoxes,* it said. And beneath that, a name. She sounded it out: "Fran-z Kaf-ka."

Their mother did not take her seat, but stood at the head of the picnic table, fumbled through the pages until she found what she was looking for, cleared her throat ceremoniously, and read:

> ***My Destination***
>
> *I gave orders for my horse to be brought round from the stable. The servant did not understand me. I myself went to the stable, saddled my horse and mounted. In the distance I heard a bugle call, I asked him what this meant. He knew nothing and had heard nothing. At the gate he stopped me, asking: "Where are you riding to, master?" "I don't know," I said, "only away from here, away from here. Always away from here, only by doing so can I reach my destination." "And so you know your destination?" he asked. "Yes," I answered, "didn't I say so? Away-From-Here, that is my destination." "You have no provisions with you," he said. "I need none," I said, "the journey is so long that I must*

> *die of hunger if I don't get anything on the way. No provisions can save me. For it is, fortunately, a truly immense journey."*

She looked up from the page, exclamation marks shooting from her eyes. There were little spots of color high on her cheeks and her hair had come a bit loose, side wisps curling in the warmth of the kitchen.

"Oh Jo," said Rav Harriett. She, too, looked electrified.

"Errrrr," said Danny. "Huh?"

"'No *provisions* can save me,'" their mother recited, adding her own emphasis. "'For it is, *fortunately,* a truly immense journey.'"

To which Rav Harriett replied, exultant, "The snake, *unfortunately,* has all its needs *provided* for."

Danny spread his fingers as if to catch an invisible ball. "Still don't get it."

"I do," said Annamae.

They turned to her, varying degrees of encouragement and skepticism on their faces.

"It makes sense because," she started bravely, never mind that her cheeks were burning, never mind that she didn't know how to say what she meant, that this, *this* was the explanation for why she couldn't do Mrs. Altschuler's assignment, not to mention the reason she'd always hated playing with dolls, because what kind of life would that be for the snake, to have everything already taken care of, with nothing to wonder about, nothing to desire, no need to reach toward anything at all? To *reach,* like Ms. Jules had said long ago. The snake in the story was doomed to be like one of those shadow puppets Nana had taken them to see, a flat thing, not really alive. Except no! She smacked her forehead with the heel of her hand. The snake had it worse, because those puppets had been treated as spiritual beings! And given offerings of dried flowers and sweets! Oh, it was impossible to squeeze it all into language. It was like trying to fit everything she thought, everything she felt, everything she believed and wished, or wish-believed, onto the teeny piece of paper inside the message-in-a-bottle necklace.

When she finished, the kitchen was quiet.

It was Danny who ended the silence, and what he said was a great deal worse because of how gently he broke it to her: "No one can understand what you're trying to say."

Postcard

Annamae began seeing Rav Harriett in her office once a week. Nobody said it was therapy, and nobody said it was preparing for her bat mitzvah, although it seemed possible it was a little of both.

Annamae had never known Rav Harriett had an office. Or that she was a therapist. Or that you could be both a rabbi and a therapist.

"I thought you worked in the hospital," she said, standing at the windowsill where Rav Harriett kept her car collection. Little metal cars, each a different color.

"I work there part-time."

Annamae had never been inside a hospital, not even when Nana had her tiny stroke. It was so tiny, she wasn't there long enough for them to visit her. Annamae had been disappointed. She was curious to know what a hospital was like. In her mind, it was blindingly, uniformly white, except for Rav Harriett with her reddish curls and candy-colored yarmulke, traveling its corridors, bringing good cheer.

Annamae liked arranging the cars in different configurations. In a row side by side, like a parking lot. In a line, like when the radio says bumper-to-bumper traffic. In a pinwheel, each car poised to drive off in a different direction, getting farther and farther from the others forever. Unless the universe was curved. Then eventually they'd crisscross.

"Mr. T. says sound waves keep traveling forever. He's our science teacher. Light waves, too. He says there could be a world just like ours existing in space and we don't realize it because it's too far away. I mean, how would we? Unless there's some other kind of signal, something that travels faster than sound and light. Or some kind of shortcut. Another way for us to know." Absentmindedly, she put the message-in-a-bottle charm in her mouth.

She was picking up the habit from Rav Harriett of saying whatever popped into her head. Often, Rav Harriett listened without feeling the need to say something back. Then Annamae would say the next thing that popped into her head.

The thing that popped into her head now was, "I have to go to the bathroom."

"Do you know where it is?"

Annamae shook her head. She was embarrassed. She'd been trying to hold it in.

Rav Harriett took a key off a hook by the door of her office and walked Annamae down the carpeted hall, past doors to other offices, all of them shut. This was her fourth time coming to Rav Harriett's office, but her first time using the bathroom. "You'll find your own way back? I'll leave my office door open."

It was more like a bathroom in somebody's house than in an office building. There was a table in one corner with potted ferns and an electric kettle and a big pair of green rubber boots underneath. The tile floor had black dots and white octagons, a pattern that could make you pleasantly dizzy if you wanted to stare long enough. While Annamae was washing her hands, she studied the dozen or so postcards decorating the wall next to the sink. They looked like they'd come from a museum gift shop. There was a sculpture, an etching, a landscape, an abstract, a still life. Then her breath stopped. It was her drawing. The one she'd found in the book at Art Explorers, the one of the two hands drawing each other, each inventing the other.

She dried her own hands and put a finger experimentally

under a corner of the postcard. It was only on there with a curl of masking tape. She peeled it carefully off the wall. It wasn't planned or thought, just something her body did.

Now there was an empty space with a little tan mark where the tape had been. So what? Lots of people used this bathroom. A postcard isn't expensive.

The postcard didn't fit in her pocket and she didn't want to bend it, so she slid it under her sweater, against her stomach, and went back to Rav Harriett's office.

How hot it was in Rav Harriett's office. The radiator gurgled. Annamae felt sweaty. The radiator banged. Annamae jumped. Rav Harriett looked at the radiator and said, "Excuse you!" and looked back at Annamae as if expecting her to laugh at the joke.

Instead, queasily, Annamae reached under her sweater and held out the postcard. "I found this."

Rav Harriett took the postcard, looked at it. "Escher," she said, nodding. She looked up.

For a pretty long time it was silent. Annamae felt like her insides were crumbling. Her eyes swam. Her nose began to drip and she wiped it a couple times with the back of her hand, and then with her cuff, but still it ran.

"There're tissues on the table."

Annamae took a few tissues and used them on her nose, then her eyes.

"Would you tell me about it?" asked Rav Harriett.

She tried. She told about Leslie and the afternoon she'd been the only student at Art Explorers and how she'd tried being funny to impress Leslie but had wound up feeling stupid and ashamed, and then how later Leslie had sat with her on the floppy couch and they'd looked through the book of drawings. Then she told about the books they'd made in Art Explorers, with the inserts that were like folding staircases and you could add as many as you liked, and she told about Coco, the leather book she'd gotten when she turned seven, and how Coco was short for Company and Coco really had accompanied her for years, how she'd made it last by gluing in paper stairs that opened up and down from the regular pages. But how even Coco wasn't real company because she, Annamae, was the only one who put anything in it. Even when she wrote conversations, dialogues, all the voices were only hers.

She told about Carla and Renu and the need for a friend, and about Nana's penny game, and Danny's letter game, and Leslie's idea game, and about the mirror she'd glued to the cover of Coco and how before going to sleep she'd sometimes study herself in that slip of glass and wish for her reflection to say something on its own. With words she didn't put in its mouth. And it never did. She told about how it was no good making things up if they weren't going to be really alive, if you were just going to make all the decisions yourself, how then it wasn't creating something real, something that belonged to itself and could have a different idea and argue with you or surprise you or love you. It was just pretend. And what was the good of that? It was too terrible, too lonely.

When Annamae stopped talking, everything was quiet. She was struck by how quiet everything was, the window, the pinwheel of metal cars, the cardboard tissue box, the rug. She put the message-in-a-bottle charm back in her mouth and worried it with her tongue.

"Do you know the story"—when Rav Harriett spoke, it was in her regular, nice, scratchy, sour-pickle voice, as if nothing Annamae had said was alarming to her—"of God consulting the angels about whether or not to create human beings?"

She shook her head.

So Rav Harriett proceeded to tell her how the angels all say, *No, no, don't do it—humans will just mess things up, cause all sorts of problems, and anyway, why create humans when you have us? We who are perfect, and incapable of sin?*

"But of course," said Rav Harriett, "God goes ahead and creates humans anyway. And do you know why? At least according to some versions of the story?"

"Why?"

"I think you have an idea."

Nodding, she said, "It's like with the snake."

From Rav Harriett's face, this was clearly not what she'd been expecting.

"The snake," explained Annamae, "from Adam and Eve."

This produced no more sign of comprehension.

"It's the thing you said, that if the snake eats dust, it has everything taken care of. It doesn't get to need anything; it doesn't get to wish for anything. It's like a doll; it's like—not really alive."

"It sounds like you're talking about free will."

Annamae, who did not know that term, nodded the more vigorously because it was novel and because it sounded just right. "Yes! And so the snake is like the angels."

"Because . . ."

Poor Rav Harriett, to need so much explaining. And still she was a hundred times closer to understanding than anyone else. "Because. You said the angels are perfect. They're incapable of sin. They don't mess up. They don't learn. They don't grow."

Rav Harriett, squinting, nodded slowly, slowly. "They, too, lack free will."

"Like dolls."

"Like dolls," agreed Rav Harriett. "Or fictional characters."

"They're not *company*." It came out very low. Tears burned in her eyes. Not because she was sad but because someone finally understood.

"Annamae, that's just what the sages say. About why God invented humans and free will, with all the mess that comes of it. Angels make for lonely company."

No one spoke or felt any need to for a while then.

When at last Annamae did, it was to ask, "Can I keep the postcard?"

"No," said the rabbi. "It isn't mine to give. One of my colleagues put them up."

And in the remaining minutes before Annamae's mother came to get her, they went down the hall together and with a fresh piece of tape stuck the postcard back on the wall.

Stranger

That night, Annamae fished Coco from her bedside table for the first time in a long time. It had somehow migrated to the bottom of a slightly teetery stack that included the pale brown workbook for practicing the letters of the *alef-bet* (everything after the first two pages was blank), the book she'd made in Art Explorers (all the pages were blank and the cover had come unglued), an Agatha Christie mystery Nana had given her for her birthday, a graphic novel Danny had lent her, and several library books, which made their crackly plastic-film sound when she moved them.

She gave herself a ritual gaze in the mirror that was no bigger than a stick of gum, then undid the thong around the middle and let the book bloom open. On the inside front cover, in big, careful childish letters that slanted up the page, it said ANNAMAE GALINKSY AGE 7 YEARS OLD. The first *E* had four horizontal lines, the second had five, and the third had three.

Leafing through the book, she found poems consisting of nothing but the words *Yes* and *No*. She found lists of names, some she recognized, like Wasim and Nobomi and Freddie Festano, and others that did not ring a bell. There were entries about things familiar to her through years of retelling, entries about things she recalled only upon being reminded, and others that meant nothing whatsoever to her now. Some passages she could make neither head nor tail of. She came across odd little drawings in crayon and colored pencil, many paper staircases she could stretch out along their folds, a page on which she'd glued flower petals, another on which she'd left a thumbprint in blood, gone rusty brown with age.

The longer she looked, the more somber she became. This object, which she'd carried around with her the way other kids might carry a blanket or a bear, this book, once her most intimate, most animate companion, had become a rather shabby thing, its cover stained, some of the stitching come loose, and—most troubling of all—much of its contents turned to gobbledygook.

Whoever had written these things was a stranger to her now.

Unseen

"It's like she's not-me."

Annamae was trying to explain to Rav Harriett the sadness of encountering the person who'd written in Coco. The childish handwriting she couldn't read, the words she could read but whose meaning had become obscure. She thought of the relationship between her actual mother and the long-ago girl who'd put stickers and scribbles on the dollhouse. It was like that. Whoever had filled the pages of Coco was at once intimately known to her and someone she could never hope to meet.

Rav Harriett put her palms together and leaned forward, a posture Annamae had come to understand as *I'm not quite grasping it, but I'm on my way. I'm en route to where you are.*

Annamae heaved her knapsack up onto the couch where she always sat in Rav Harriett's office. Rav Harriett, across from her in the purple armchair, said, "What do they make you carry, rocks?"

"No, I brought . . ." She dug through the bag, shoving aside textbooks and spirals and her empty lunch box, hunting for the little leather-bound book. "I wanted to show you . . ." She'd packed it that morning for the very purpose of bringing it to Rav Hariett's office. "I know I put it . . ."

But it wasn't there.

"Maybe it's at school?"

Annamae shook her head, trying not to cry. "I never took it out of my knapsack."

"Maybe you'll find it when you get home."

Annamae bit the inside of her mouth hard.

"It might really be lost," said Rav Harriett.

Annamae was—not relieved, but, yes, grateful that Rav Harriett said out loud what was hard but true.

"Annamae. What would that mean to you?"

For some reason, what came into her head was the nursery rhyme Nobomi used to sing them: *"Umzi watsha,"* about the house on fire.

"What," asked Rav Harriett, "are you feeling right now?"

Annamae turned her palms up helplessly. And began to talk. In a low voice. To explain how she felt. Once she'd had this book, Coco, in whom she'd confided her deepest, rawest, most unapologetic and unintelligible soul. And now at age twelve, she had moved beyond the realm of being able to grasp, to perceive and love what her younger self had written. It was the ultimate betrayal: her inability to read the marks, the messages, made by her own hand.

Rav Harriett was silent long enough that Annamae began to worry she was no longer en route. Then she made one of her by-now-familiar conversational leaps. "You know what the Torah is?"

Annamae gave a one-shouldered shrug.

"It's—well, it's a lot of things, but one of the things we mean when we say *Torah* is the Hebrew Bible, specifically the teachings that God delivered to Moses on Mount Sinai. And the tradition is that the original Torah wasn't written with ink on parchment, or even letters chiseled into stone, but with fire. Black fire written on white fire. Are you with me? Kind of?"

". . . Kind of."

"So the—*I* think—pretty astonishing thing in our

tradition is that the white fire is even more important than the black fire. All the blank spaces on the page where there *isn't* writing, where we see nothing. The part we can't read, that's considered the highest part. The closest to God part, if you believe in God, or to the universe, if you prefer. To all that's unknowable. Beyond us."

Annamae pulled out her bottom lip.

"Is this—are you not with me?"

"White fire, black fire . . ."

"'Enough about the Torah—what does this have to do with me?'"

Annamae tried unsuccessfully to suppress a smile.

"I understand that looking through the pages of your old journal—"

"Notebook."

"—your old notebook, Coco, I understand you weren't feeling connected to the writing in it. And that that's troubling." She paused for confirmation.

Annamae nodded.

"But the book still feels important to you." Another pause.

Another nod.

"So what I'm wondering is—maybe," said Rav Harriett—Annamae loved how searching she sounded, how halting and determined, as if they were standing on an uncertain shore and she was foraging for words, assembling and loading them one by one onto a raft that might ferry them to the other side—"maybe your connection doesn't have to be through the part that's written. Maybe the connection is in the part you can't see."

Luck

When they learned about Nana's tiny stroke, Annamae had wondered aloud, "Does this mean she's going to die?"

"No," said Danny. "She was always going to die. So are you, by the way."

"Hey." Their mother put a hand on Danny's shoulder. To Annamae: "I think you're asking if she's going to die from this?"

"Or if not from this, exactly . . . does it mean she's on her way?"

"To dying?"

"We're all on our way to dying," said Danny.

Their mother gave his shoulder a shake.

"What?" said Danny. "It's scientifically true."

"I understand you may be feeling upset," said their mother. "Don't take it out on your sister." To Annamae: "You're wondering if this is a sign that she's getting close to dying?"

"Yes."

"The doctors say there's no reason to think that. Her stroke was the mildest kind."

"How do you know?"

"Science," said Danny.

"They have tests that measure these things. It was very mild. She was lucky."

"Dumb luck," said Annamae.

Sharply, as if Annamae had said something naughty, her mother said, "What?"

"That's what Nana calls it. 'Pure dumb luck.'"

And Annamae realized something. Her mother, and Danny, and just about everyone she knew, seemed to prefer it when things could be measured and mapped by science. She, alone perhaps, preferred it when they could not. Her comfort lay in things that fell into the category of luck. The random and the strange. Things that pointed toward an existence no one could explain. The single pane that showed blue sky when all the others showed snow.

Angels

They went to the museum to see the Christmas tree. They themselves never had a Christmas tree, although every year at this time their mother did string tiny colored lights on the potted grapefruit. When they had been little, she used to serve them breakfast by candlelight from the winter solstice until daylight saving time resumed.

"Why don't we do that anymore?" griped Annamae.

"I guess the novelty wore off."

"Maybe for you."

It was the first week in January, the last week the tree would be on display. It had snowed a lot, then turned unseasonably warm. Everywhere lay puddles or mounds of gray slush. The museum was packed. "To the gills," declared Nana, who was with them. The trip was in a way for Nana, who had taken their mother to see the tree every year when she had been a kid.

"Apparently, *that* novelty didn't wear off," mumbled Annamae.

"What?"

"Nothing."

Even though Nana was supposedly all better, it had still taken her a long time to go up all the salt-strewn granite steps to the entrance, holding on to the railing with one hand and on to Danny's friend Dante's elbow with the other. Dante had come with them, too. They were quite a crowd (their mother had declared as much—"We're quite a crowd!"—once they were finally inside and waiting in line to buy tickets with a thousand other people, all of them sweating in their winter coats): Nana, their mother, Danny, Dante, Annamae, and Felice. Felice was there as Annamae's friend.

"You can each invite a friend," their mother had told them the day before. It was clearly meant to preempt their saying, Do we have to go?

"I don't have a friend."

"Why don't you ask one of the kids from your birthday party?"

Felice had been available. She'd gotten dropped off at their apartment the next morning wearing a museumy outfit that included a purse worn diagonally across her coat and new fur-lined boots.

"Your feet are going to be hot," said Annamae.

"No they won't," said Felice. "It's faux."

Instead of the subway they'd taken an Uber, because of Nana, all of them squished into an SUV that had deposited them right in front of the museum. Now in line inside, they were barely less squished. "Think how much worse it would've been if we'd come during school vacation," said their mother.

Think how much better it would've been if you didn't make us come at all popped into Annamae's head, although she didn't say it. Possibly she didn't even mean it.

At last they reached the room with the great blue spruce. Around the base was a diorama populated with fantastically molded people and animals all come to see the newborn baby and his parents. Above them, the branches held dozens of angels and what looked like electric birthday candles. On every side you could hear sighs of *How beautiful!* and people pointing out exquisite details to one another. "There's a fisherman with a fish." "See the tiny dagger tucked in that one's belt?" "Look, this guy has bagpipes."

"Oh my God, the cherubs!" said Felice. She put her mouth close to Annamae's ear. "You can see their exact penises."

A woman behind them with a voice like a duchess remarked to her companion, "Isn't it remarkable the way each one is unique?"

The angels wore colored silks that had been stiffened with wire to make it appear they were billowing on the nonexistent breeze. Their wings were as expressive and distinct as their faces. The longer she looked, the more she noticed. One she could practically hear gasping. One looked a bit smug, like a game-show host saying, "Ta da!" One looked mid-swoon. One was so tender-eyed, so brimming with calm, knowing adoration, it made Annamae wish she were the baby Jesus.

"Which is your favorite?" asked Felice. "Mine's that one in the pink. With the silver thingy in her hand."

"I don't really care for angels," said Annamae.

"Annamae! Oh my God, Annamae—why not?"

Because, thought Annamae, like the snake, they have no lack. Aloud she said, "Because they look down on us."

Felice gave her a little whack on the arm with her purse. "You. Are. So. Extra!" She dissolved into peals of laughter. She had a laugh that made people look over and smile.

Annamae felt something like laughter bubble up inside her, too. She forced herself to concentrate on the blue spruce, the ancient angels, their bare feet, their expressive toes. "I like their toes," she allowed.

Felice bent double at that.

Not Exactly

But it was not exactly true, said Rav Harriett when Annamae told her about this exchange.

Angels were not just one thing.

There were lots of different stories about angels. And even in just that one story they'd talked about, the one where God is asking the angels whether or not to create human beings, there were lots of different interpretations. Some of the sages said God asked their opinion out of real ambivalence. (Annamae: "A question of curiosity.") Some said God wanted to demonstrate that it's good to be humble. Some said the angels themselves disagreed about how to respond.

The angel of love said, *Yes, create people, because they'll do acts of kindness.* The angel of truth said, *No, don't, because they'll just lie.* The angel of righteousness said, *Yes, do, because people will work for justice.* The angel of peace said, *No, no, no; they're just going to fight all the time.*

"It's true," observed Annamae.

"Which?"

"Well. All of it."

Rav Harriett grinned.

Annamae frowned.

"What?"

"It's just. If they're all saying different things and they're all right, it's . . ."

"Yes?"

"Frustrating."

Rav Harriett clapped her hands together. "You know what'll bug you even more?" She said it like Ooh, do I have a treat for you! She crossed the office to the bookshelf behind her desk. When she found what she was looking for, she carried it over not to the purple armchair where she always sat, but to the couch, planting herself thigh to thigh with Annamae and opening the book so that it spread over both their laps. This reminded Annamae so vividly of the time Leslie had shown her the big book of Escher drawings that for an instant she wondered if Rav Harriett and Leslie were really the same person. Then instantly she was embarrassed because, obviously. That was stupid.

Anyway, this book was totally different. Annamae had never seen anything like it. In the middle of the page was a box of writing, bordered by columns of more writing, and those columns were surrounded on all sides by still more blocks of text. The letters were all from the *alef-bet,* so she couldn't read what it said. But the layout, like a patchwork quilt or a hedge maze, might have been something out of Escher.

"This is the Talmud. Or a fraction of it." Rav Harriett said the whole Talmud consisted of sixty-three tractates.

"What're tractates?"

Tractates were kind of like volumes, she said, and they covered all sorts of subjects: law, history, ethics, folklore. "Just about everything under the sun. There's stuff in here about farming." Rav Harriett turned the pages slowly. Annamae saw how the arrangement varied from page to page, how the hedge maze did not replicate itself exactly, but shifted its pattern. "Stuff on health care. Cooking. Fashion. Philosophy. Jokes."

"How come it looks like that?"

Rav Harriett said it showed you who was talking. The different sections represented different sages' opinions about the writing in the center. "Remember I was telling you about the black fire and the white fire?"

Annamae nodded.

"So all this white space between the blocks of text—and even within the blocks of text, right? *all* the white space—that's the most important part. That openness makes room for our questions, and it's also what allows all these sages to gather. In a sense. Some of them lived hundreds of years apart, right? They never got to meet in real life. But here they get to be in conversation with one another. Disputing across the ages."

"Disputing." Annamae tasted the word. "So it's like a book of arguments?"

"Arguments. Tangents. Measurements. Refinements. Disagreements."

"Who wins?"

"Who wins what?"

"Like on this page, each of these"—tapping her finger on the outer quadrilaterals—"is a different opinion about what that"—the innermost quadrilateral—"means?"

"Yes."

"So how do you know which one is right?"

"The short answer is, you don't. The slightly less short answer is, that's what keeps it juicy. That's why people still read it, still study it, still, for that matter, keep arguing about it, to this very day. It's for each of us, in every generation, to interpret for ourselves."

Annamae scratched her nose. "But, you know. What do the top people say is right?"

"Top people?"

"Like the Pope?"

"We don't have a Pope."

"But *like* the Pope. The head rabbis or whatever."

Rav Harriett gave her head a little shake. "We don't have a central authority figure."

"What about God?"

There was a silence. Annamae felt proud to have come up with such a deep, wise response.

Rav Harriett drew a long breath through her nose. "Oh Annamae," she said. "What a very good question that is."

Annamae tried to look modest. She imagined Rav Harriett saying, Of course. She imagined Rav Harriett smacking herself on the forehead and saying, Yes, you're right. How could I have missed it—God! She imagined the rabbi from Shayna's bat mitzvah saying, Annamae is a very special girl.

Rav Harriett frowned out the window, as if a million thoughts were fluttering around inside her head and she had to hold very still in order to let them flock together and assume a clear shape.

Outside the window, the city had grown dark. Actually, no. It had become a relief map of light: The lit grid of office windows, the glow of storefronts at street level, the headlights creeping sluggishly along the avenue, all of these stood out from the thickening shadows.

When next she spoke, Rav Harriett said (what else?), "That reminds me of a story."

Akhnai's Oven

The sages are sitting around the study house discussing the oven of Akhnai. It's a new invention, an oven made of baked tiles held together with unbaked mortar. This way, it's portable; it can easily be taken apart and moved and reassembled. What the sages are trying to figure out is if this oven counts as a vessel, in which case it has to be ritually purified each time it's assembled. Or does the fact that it's made up of separate pieces mean it's not a true vessel and therefore it's exempt?

"This is the kind of thing the sages could get really into," Rav Harriett said.

Rabbi Eliezer says it doesn't count as a vessel, so they don't need to worry about purifying it. The others all say no, it is a vessel, and therefore requires ritual purification. Rabbi Eliezer explains all the logical, scientific reasons why he's right, but he can't get any of the other sages on board. Finally, he resorts to nonlogical, nonscientific reasons. He says, "Look, let me prove it to you. If I'm right, let this carob tree give a sign." Sure enough, the carob tree gets up and moves to a different spot.

Astonishing as that is, the other sages won't concede the point.

So Rabbi Eliezer says, "Not good enough for you? Okay: If I'm right, let this stream over here give a sign." Sure enough, the stream starts flowing in the opposite direction.

Mind-boggling, but the other sages? Still unconvinced.

Then Rabbi Eliezer says, "Really? Wow. Fine. If I'm

right, let the very walls of this study house give a sign." And lo and behold, the walls start to crumble around them.

One of the other sages, Rabbi Yehoshua, scolds the walls. He tells them not to get involved. Chastened, they stop crumbling. But out of respect for Rabbi Eliezer, they don't go back to their original position, either.

"This," said Rav Harriett, "is what we call a 'sight gag.'"

Even so, the sages refuse to believe that Rabbi Eliezer is right.

So he calls in the big guns: "If I'm right, let Heaven prove it!"

On cue, a Divine Voice calls down: "Why are you disagreeing with Rabbi Eliezer when he's right?"

And Rabbi Yehoshua says—to God, he says this—"With all due respect, please stay out of it. You gave the Torah to us; You left it up to us to interpret for ourselves. So at this point? It's not really up to You."

"You know what happens then?" Rav Harriett asked.

Annamae shook her head.

"God smiles this big delighted smile and says, 'My children! My children have triumphed over me!'"

Etymology

Nobomi was getting married and Annamae wasn't invited.

"No kids are invited, honey," her mother explained.

Annamae sat on the floor by the coffee table, fingering the invitation. It consisted of three envelopes (a big outer, a medium inner, and an adorable little baby one to mail back), two cards (the invitation itself and the RSVP), and two pieces of tissue paper, which were somehow the best part. That, and the gold foil envelope liner.

"Are you going?"

"Yes."

"Can I fill out the RSVP card?"

"No."

"I'll write very neatly."

"No."

"Why not?"

"I don't know, Annamae. I'm feeling pressured." Her mother spoke in a warning tone of voice. She was sitting in the blue armchair with her laptop on a pillow on her stomach, working on their taxes.

"Do I have taxes?"

"Eh, kind of. You're part of mine. When you have a job, you'll have your own taxes."

"Felice has a job."

"Mm?"

"She babysits three days a week for twins in her building."

"How old?"

"Felice?"

"The twins."

"I don't know. Four."

"Oof."

"Felice is turning thirteen already. In a month."

"Mm."

"Why did you go 'Oof'?"

"Two four-year-olds sounds like a lot of work."

"Do taxes have anything to do with ataxia?"

Her mother looked up from the laptop. "Are you being funny?" She was highly sensitive around the subject of Nana lately.

Annamae had intended it as a joke, but now she said, "No, I mean ety-mo-logically." She wasn't a linguist's daughter for nothing.

"Oh."

"Is it?"

"I have no idea. Look it up."

"Can I at least have the pieces of tissue paper?"

"What?"

"The pieces of tissue paper. From the thingy." Annamae held up the pieces of tissue paper from the wedding invitation.

"No."

"Why not?"

"Oh Annamae. Fine."

Annamae pressed one of the pieces of tissue paper to her mouth like a lady blotting lipstick on TV. It stuck there and wagged interestingly when next she moved her mouth. "I can't believe we're not invited."

No sound from the armchair but keyboard pitter-patter.

"Me and Danny," she clarified, dangling the bad grammar like a mouse in front of a cat.

Her mother did not pounce.

"You know God likes it when people tell Him to butt out? It cracks Him up."

This did not get a rise, either.

Annamae let out a long groan. "I'm soooo bored," she groaned, flopping sideways on the rug.

"You don't say," murmured her mother, typing away.

Ventriloquist

Felice's mom was going on a date. She was only going out within the same building. Felice and her mom lived on the seventeenth floor. Kate, the date, lived on the third. Annamae was there to keep Felice company so her mom didn't have to feel guilty. That's how Felice explained it when she invited Annamae to sleep over.

"I know it's probably a bad idea to date someone in the building," Felice's mom muttered as she checked herself in the mirror by the door.

"It's convenient," offered Felice.

"My chief criteria in a romantic partner."

"Don't wear those earrings," said Felice.

"Which ones should I wear?"

"Literally any others."

Felice's mom angled her head left, then right, looking in the mirror. Dangly wooden peace signs. "No, I like these," she muttered. "How's my lipstick?"

"You need more. It doesn't even look like you're wearing any."

"Good," muttered Felice's mom.

Annamae was coming to realize that was just the way she talked. She had a way of not really moving her mouth. She would make a good ventriloquist.

"All right, girls. Wish me luck. Text if anything catches fire."

"Good luck," said Felice. "Not that you need it."

Felice's mom, halfway out the door, turned back. "Aw!"

She blew them kisses. "I'm so glad you're here, Annamae, to keep Felice company! Have fun!"

Felice put a finger to her lips and beckoned Annamae over to the closed door, where they stood listening to Felice's mom sing "The Surrey with the Fringe on Top" until the elevator came. Felice raised her eyebrows at Annamae and pantomimed dying of laughter.

For supper they had individual chicken potpies and root beer floats. Felice took a bottle from a cabinet over the sink and poured some on top of each of their floats. She said it was cherry syrup. It tasted of medicine.

After, they tried on clothes from Felice's mom's closet. "I don't think we should be doing this," said Annamae as Felice's head emerged from the neck of a pistachio silk blouse.

"She doesn't mind as long as we're careful."

They took turns modeling outfits in front of the long freestanding mirror in the bedroom. Through the window beyond the mirror shone the lights of other apartment buildings, tiny squares against the darkness, a geometry of other lives. Annamae found a crushed velvet jacket the color of ginger ale. The cuffs came way past her hands. Felice rolled them up for her. "You look good," she said, her reflection meeting Annamae's in the eye.

Annamae felt shimmery inside, like a column of heat vapor. She had a dim memory of a time when she'd leapt on the sidewalk while watching her reflection in a shop window, and she'd seen not one but two bodies leaping in the glass. One leaping a split second after the other.

But was that true?

What if I'm not me? thought Annamae. Or what if I'm not only me? What if these thoughts I'm thinking aren't mine, but only seem that way? What if someone else put them in my head? Will we ever meet?

Feeling hot and dizzy, she bent toward the mirror until

her forehead touched the glass. She let her reflection slip out of focus. Kissed herself on the cool, hard lips.

"What's the matter with you?" asked Felice.

"Nothing." She couldn't shake the thought that she might be unreal. What if she was only somebody else's invention? And everything she said was only a ventriloquist's voice speaking through her. "Blah blah blah," she said, hoping to break the spell.

"Are you going to barf?" Matter-of-factly, Felice instructed, "If you're going to barf, make sure you take off the jacket first."

Travesty

She would not cave. She would not invent characters that had no life but that which she designed for them. In the end, Mrs. Altschuler struck a deal with her. Annamae could do the assignment as nonfiction instead of fiction. She still had to do all the parts—Character Building Worksheets, Paragraphs of Detailed Description, Vignettes With Action—but she would be allowed to describe real people, real events. She also still had to turn everything in by the end of the quarter, which meant she had to do in eleven days what everyone else had done in ten weeks.

"I hate this," she informed her mother.

"Be that as it may." Her mother was toasting spices in a little cast-iron skillet while Annamae sat at the table with her folder and worksheets and notebook and pen and colored pencils.

"Be that as it may, what?"

"Be that as it may, get it done."

"What are you making?"

"Berbere."

"It smells."

"Annamae."

"What? It smells good."

It did smell good. It smelled like brown-and-gold plaid. Annamae tried to draw the smell in her notebook. She'd gotten out her colored pencils because one of the options on the worksheets was to draw your characters. She did not want to draw her characters any more than she wanted to write down their Physical Attributes and Traits. She had tried multiple times, and each drawing came out more of a travesty than the last.

That was a Felice word. Felice, standing in front of the mirror, taking a thousand years to arrange and rearrange the same two barrettes, was fond of declaring, "My hair is a travesty."

The kitchen garbage, as well as the slanting floor all around it, was currently littered with Annamae's crumpled travesties.

"Kill some trees, why don't you?" said Danny, coming into the kitchen. "What're you drawing?" He bent over her shoulder, trying to see.

Annamae rounded her body over the notebook. "Ugh, Danny. Your breath."

Danny went over to the garbage, plucked out the topmost reject, smoothed it, and studied the drawing. "What's this supposed to be?" Merrily: "Is this supposed to be Dante?" Then even more merrily: "Is this supposed to be *me*?"

"You're such an ass, Danny. I know that one's no good. That's why it's in the trash. For your info."

"Danny, let her work."

"What?" Little disbelieving laugh sounds from Danny. He sounded like a cat trying to cough up a fur ball. "What am I even doing?"

"Danny."

"Fine." He recrumpled her drawing and chucked it back in the garbage.

"Mom!" Annamae shrieked.

"What did he do?"

"What did I do?"

"He threw away my paper!"

"I put it back where I found it!" Danny swatted the side of Annamae's head. She leapt from the bench and flung herself at him, and then they were on the floor, the two of them, far too old, at twelve and fourteen, for such behavior. When they stopped—breaking off awkwardly after less than a minute of pounding and shoving, as if they themselves were appalled to have wound up in pitched battle—their mother was in tears, and the coriander, fenugreek, and cardamom seeds were scorched.

Machloket

"*Machloket l'shem shamayim*," said Rav Harriett after a pause. This was her response to Annamae's telling her about the fight with Danny.

"Huh?" said Annamae. She made a special effort to say it humorously, because the mood in Rav Harriett's little book-choked office high above the avenue had grown solemn. Telling about the fight, and her mother's tears, and the burnt spices had made something clench in Annamae's throat and she'd abruptly stopped talking and plucked a tissue from the box on the table, just in case.

"Argument for the sake of heaven."

"Huh?"

"It's something Rebbe Nachman said. Reb Nachman of Breslov. He said *machloket*, disputes between scholars, opens up a necessary space." Rav Harriett expanded her palms around an invisible balloon being inflated.

"Why necessary?"

"I think what he meant is that if everyone agreed on everything, if there was total oneness"—now bringing her palms together and interlacing her fingers—"there'd be no room. We *need* the space opened up by difference, by division"—she let her palms drift apart again—"for creativity. Without such a space, creation could never occur."

"Like the big bang," said Annamae. Eerily, Mr. T. had done the exact same thing with his hands, showing them how the universe began. He had a big bang poster taped to the side of the supply cabinet. It was literally a picture of the big bang, he said. An actual photograph of leftover light.

Annamae looked down at the just-in-case tissue wadded in her hands. She unwadded it, then teased apart the corner and separated it into two thinner tissues. Thin as skin, thin as veils. She wondered if Nobomi was going to wear a wedding veil. A wedding brought people together, but it also drew them away from other people. It split things up. In her mind she saw Freddie Festano run his electric carving knife between her and Nobomi the way he'd run it down the center of the foam rubber mattress. She saw Renu being cleaved from the city, then drifting through space back to Pittsburgh. She saw Carla being whisked from her desk and carried backward, as if by a wind, to the class for kids who needed extra help. She saw the copper penny leap from her hand and go flipping over and over toward the hole in the sewer cover. She saw a girl opening a hinged dollhouse, splitting the sides apart. The girl looked up, met her eyes, and vanished.

Plaques

Felice had a thing about plaques.

"Plaque?" Annamae thought of the dentist.

"Plaques! Plaques!"

"You sound like a duck," said Annamae.

Felice, committed to her complaint, did not crack a smile. "They're everywhere. It's ridiculous."

Thanks to Felice, Annamae had begun spotting plaques all over the city. On buildings, embedded in the sidewalk, screwed into park benches. Plaques on streetlamps and plaques in the subway. Some in memory of a person who had died. Some in memory of a business or school or synagogue that once stood on a certain spot. Some marking a particular event. Where a famous person had been born. Where a battle had been fought. Where the first moving picture had been projected. Where cotton had been exchanged, poems written, human beings bought and sold. Where an uprising had started. Where someone had proposed marriage. Where a pear tree, now dead and gone, once bore fruit.

"But why do you think they're ridiculous?" asked Annamae when, weeks later, Felice reprised her theme.

They were sitting on a park bench with a plaque—not graffiti, an actual metal plaque—inscribed First Kiss * 7/3/83 * M.J. & F.K. It was one of the first warm days and they had ambitiously worn tank tops. Annamae was chilly, but a guy came by and asked if they wanted to buy weed, which made Felice declare it was worth it.

Annamae didn't see why.

"It means we look old," Felice explained. Her tank top was made of white eyelet. She had turned thirteen a week ago. Instead of a party her mother and her mother's girlfriend had taken her out for steak and lobster.

"Why do we want to look old?"

"Not *old* old. Just older than we are. Sophisticated."

The park smelled like burning rope and green shoots and wet stones and caramelized nuts and exhaust fumes.

"Well anyway, why do you think plaques are ridiculous?" Annamae's tank top was a hand-me-down from Danny. It was black, with *Slam Dunk Academy* written in orange.

"Because," Felice said, "they're superfluous." That had been a word on their vocabulary test. She spread her two bare brown arms across the top of the park bench, tilted her face to the April sun, and closed her eyes. She was wearing eyeliner. Annamae could see where it had been applied a little inexpertly. "They're all just saying the same thing."

Annamae thought of all the different plaques she'd been noticing lately. "What do you mean? What same thing do they say?"

"Something Happened Here."

Fajitas

Annamae thought Felice might be a little bit of a genius. Or at least that she was probably right that something important to somebody must have happened, at some point in time, pretty much everywhere you looked. But Annamae did not agree about the plaques being ridiculous. She liked the idea of calling people's attention to what would otherwise remain obscure. She tried to imagine what it would look like if there really were plaques to mark all the hidden wonders. Or better—how it would be to have special glasses that let you see otherwise invisible signposts everywhere you looked.

When she told Danny and Dante about it, Dante said that what Felice actually was was an airhead.

"No she's not."

Dante laughed.

"She isn't!"

"Lighten up, Annamae." Danny set a flour tortilla on the burner. Their mother was working late, helping run a conference (Prosodic Bootstrapping in Infant Language Acquisition), and Danny and Dante were in charge of supper tonight.

"It's on fire," said Annamae.

Danny began to whistle. It took a moment for Annamae to recognize the tune as "*Umzi watsha*."

"Dude," said Dante. "She's right."

Still whistling, Danny flipped the tortilla with a pair of tongs. A few spots had bubbled and blackened. He gave the second side several seconds over the open flame, then removed the tortilla to a plate and threw another on the burner.

"Where'd you learn that?" Their mother always toasted tortillas in the oven.

"YouTube. Dante, want to stir those peppers?"

While the boys cooked the meat and peppers and onions and beans, Annamae set out the cold toppings. Grated cheese, shredded lettuce, chopped tomatoes, guacamole, sour cream. As she placed each bowl on the picnic table she thought, Something happened here, and something happened here, and something also happened here . . . as if she was practicing for something.

Or praying, almost.

It was a kind of prayer for someone who did not know how to pray.

Like that shepherd boy who just called out the letters of the *alef-bet,* trusting the message to become clear upon arrival.

"Hey, Annamae," asked Dante, "you ever get that assignment back?"

He was referring to the dreaded, dreadful creative writing unit. Upon learning that she'd chosen them as her characters, Danny and Dante had been eager to claim an advisory role. Or more than advisory; they wound up supplying her with the material. Instead of making things up, all she had to do was write down the words. They dictated everything from lists of Identifying Characteristics to Vignettes Involving Two Characters to the final Short Story, which they titled "Buzzer Beater."

"What'd you get on it?" Dante wanted to know.

"A C plus."

"Dang!"

"Points off for lateness."

He looked partially mollified.

She didn't care about the grade. She was just relieved to no longer be in the position of causing Mrs. Altschuler and her mother grief. And to have gotten through the unit without bending to its requirements.

And yet she wondered—the creative writing unit had planted within her the seeds of a question—might it be possible to create something beyond your control? To imagine something into being that yet had a life of its own, an unruliness, an ability to disobey, perhaps to invent you in return?

Havruta

When Annamae told Rav Harriett what Felice had said, and of the questions it had stirred in her, Rav Harriett asked, "Is she someone who might be your *havruta?*"

This was one of the special words Rav Harriett had taught her. It had been growing over the months, this vocabulary of shared words, almost like a code or private language between them. "A lexicon built for two," Rav Harriett once called it.

Some weeks ago she'd introduced this new word, explaining the tradition of studying the Torah in pairs. You weren't supposed to study alone, Rav Harriett had explained, but with a study partner.

"So you have somebody to fight with," Annamae said.

"Ehhhhh, primarily somebody to learn with, but yes, sure, learning may often take the form of disputation." Anyway, she'd gone on, this person who could challenge you, disagree with you, help you see things from different angles, this was called *havruta.* She'd suggested that maybe Annamae's wish for a "special friend" (using her fingers to make quotation marks in the air) was really a longing for *havruta.* Not someone who would know "the exact same things" (more quotation marks), but precisely someone who wouldn't.

"What would be so special about that?" retorted Annamae. "That's—everyone!"

Rav Harriett had laughed appreciatively. "I guess that's true. I'm not trying to suggest that everyone, or just anyone, would fit the bill. But someone who thinks exactly like you might not, either. It seems to me that would be as lonely as talking to yourself."

Now Rav Harriett suggested, "This Felice sounds like she might be a good *havruta*. What do you think?"

"If you knew her . . ." Annamae wrinkled her nose. "She's actually kind of an airhead."

Rav Harriett chuckled. "Okay. I'm not here to sell you on Felice. But can I ask you a serious question?"

Annamae made a look like *Obviously*.

"Might your longing for an idealized friend be similar to the very thing that bothered you about the English assignment?"

"What English assignment?"

"'What English assignment?'" Rav Harriett lifted her hands and dropped them heavily on her lap. "The one you refused to do, the reason you started coming to see me."

It was jarring to hear Rav Harriett be so blunt. The weird thing was, Annamae still didn't even know whether her mother was paying for these sessions. She didn't necessarily want to know. What she did know was that right now, for the first time, she felt angry at Rav Harriett. "I don't get what you're saying."

"You seem to be holding out for a soul mate who's going to think and feel exactly like you. Any deviation, in your eyes, would be a bitter disappointment. I'm asking, how is that any different from what you objected to in the creative writing assignment? There, you didn't want total control over a character. When you first started coming here, you talked about the loneliness of being the one making it all up."

Annamae picked at a hole in her jeans.

"A longing for someone identical to you, that's not relationship. That's replication."

She made the hole larger and hooked her finger through.

"I'm wondering," said Rav Harriett, "could you allow the same . . . unpredictability, the same freedom, the same possibility of surprising you that you so badly wanted your fictional characters to have—could you allow that in a friend?"

Thirst

"Yes, my friend?" said Wasim.

Annamae was meeting her mother up by her office after school. They were going shopping together for the dress her mother would wear to Nobomi's wedding.

"Let me guess," said Wasim. "Halvah bomb."

"No thank you," said Annamae. She had, in fact, approached the counter with the intention of getting a halvah bomb, but then she'd noticed the girl behind the counter and it had made her shy.

There was something about the girl. Not only the fact that she looked to be the same age. She had her back to customers, was wearing an apricot kerchief and a gray corduroy jumper. A fat brown braid stuck out of the apricot kerchief. She was folding pastry boxes and stacking them on the back shelf.

"Then . . ."

"Oh. Tea, please."

Wasim put his eyebrows up. A delicate form of foot tapping.

"Um, hibiscus, please."

With a single nod, he went to the other end of the counter.

Annamae could see only a sliver of the girl's profile, like the thinnest paring of moon. Thirsting for more, she began to hum. She was surprised by her own brazenness.

The girl glanced over her shoulder.

Annamae smiled at her.

The girl might not have seen—in any case, she just picked up a new piece of cardboard and began creasing it along the factory-made folds, tucking tabs into slits.

"Um," said Annamae. "Do you happen to have the time?"

The girl turned around. She had a perfect little mole under one eye. "What?"

"I just wondered if you have the time?"

"Baba!" The girl called down the counter. "What time is it?"

"Already, you're asking?"

"Not me, the customer."

"Ah, the customer"—Wasim brightened his voice as he came back down to Annamae's end of the counter and handed over the ruby drink—"five minutes to four."

"Thanks. Thanks," said Annamae, once for the time and once for the tea. And instead of returning to her table, she lingered there, one foot hooked behind the opposite calf. What was this thirst?

"You never met my daughter? Anam, say hello."

The girl turned from folding boxes once more. Her braid brushed across the corduroy like the tail of a cat. Instead of saying hello, she gave Annamae such a look: a kind of glower lit by knowing amusement. As if they were complicit in some dark joke.

For the next twenty minutes, Annamae sat and stirred her tea—undrinkable without the sugar she was suddenly embarrassed to add—and stole glances at the girl her own age whose name held her own syllables, who folded boxes and tamped espresso and steamed milk. Once she came around and cleared dishes from the next table, and Annamae smiled at her again, but she didn't notice.

When there was a lull, Wasim's daughter sat on a stool, bent over a book, brushing the tip of her fat brown braid back and forth across her chin.

What are you reading? Annamae wanted to ask. But that was for another world, the one in which she and Wasim's daughter become best friends. The one in which the recognition is mutual from the start. In which Wasim's daughter, from the moment she lays eyes on Annamae, opens her rib cage and beams forth light.

When at last her mother pushed through the door, briefcase-laden, jacket misbuttoned, breathless, late, Annamae was already in a foul mood.

Hunger

Helping pick out her mother's dress was meant to be a treat that might make up for, or at least soften, the injustice Annamae felt over not being invited to the wedding. It backfired. Her sense of grievance was not only intact but validated.

Now in the store every rebuffed suggestion—"What about this one?" "Oh, you should get this!" "You could at least try this one *on*"—compounded the insult.

Her mother said no to red, no to beading, no to off the shoulder, no to pleated chiffon.

Her mother said, "Hold this, please," and thrust out her briefcase like Annamae was the butler.

Her mother said, "Holy moly" as she turned over price tags.

In the fitting room, Annamae got to see her mother's body up close in sallow light. It was neither fat nor thin, just a bit lumpy. There was a bruise on her shin and scrawly bits of black hair coming out of her underwear.

"I'll wait out there."

"Oh, would you mind?" her mother implored. "I need help with the zippers."

Annamae's stomach was rumbling. "Can we go out for hamburgers after this?"

"I'm never having a hamburger again," her mother murmured. Hand on belly, inspecting herself sideways in boring navy silk.

"But seriously, can we?"

"Oh Annamae. I already defrosted the chicken."

"What chicken?"

"The chicken. From whenever. Sunday. Or Saturday. Can you unzip me?" she asked, turning her back and holding up her hair.

Despite her mood, Annamae was careful to be careful. With an earlier dress, she'd accidentally caught a bit of skin in the metal teeth and her mother had yelped. Her mother's back had so many freckles. More than she remembered. The writing on the tag on her bra had been laundered into oblivion. It hit Annamae that being invited on this shopping trip was really a chore disguised as a treat.

"But I'm really hungry," she insisted. She could already taste the warm ketchup and pickle.

"Don't whine. What did you eat at Memuzin? That's why I gave you money."

"Nothing. Just tea. I didn't even drink it."

"Well." Her mother expelled a short laugh. The navy puddled at her feet. "That was wasteful."

"Mom!" Annamae drew back as much as possible—within the confines of the fitting room, a mostly symbolic distance.

Something ugly continued to vibrate in the silence as her mother bent, put the navy dress back on its hanger, and worked the next one over her head. Beige gauze. Her hair had gone staticky. She groped for the zipper and did it up herself as far as she could. Annamae didn't step forward to help. The chest part of the dress bunched loosely and the part over the stomach stretched tight. She lifted her chest, pushed her shoulders back, and studied herself in the three-panel dressing room mirror that made hundreds of copies of her. No matter how she angled her body, they were all her, just the same. Eventually she whispered, "Good God."

What was that thing Rav Harriett had said? The loneliness of having only yourself, or someone just like you, for company. Annamae glared at her own face in the mirror. Nothing but replication as far as the eye could see.

Grief

That night, Annamae wept.

She had surprised herself earlier in the day by humming. Now she surprised herself again by crying.

From her bed, the window in her room showed the backs of the buildings on the other side of the block and little crooked bits of sky. The sky outside her window never got deeply dark the way it did at Nana's. Here in the city it just drained of color. Like when you got shaved ice in the park in the summer and you sucked all the flavored syrup out.

Annamae lay there on her sawed-apart half-queen foam rubber mattress, looking at the bits of pale, starless darkness, and something built up within her and it built up and it built up and it was a terrible ache and she began to weep in a way she'd never wept before.

The word *grief* came to her. It was such a grown-up word. It made her feel as if she were traveling into a foreign realm.

Tears coursed down both sides of her face. Sobs racked her silently. That was all. She lay there and wept without understanding. Tears wet her left ear, then pooled in her right. Soundless spasms made her abdomen jerk. These distinct functions of her body went on long enough that they became almost diverting. As if the weeping didn't originate from her but was something imposed on her body from an outside source. She pictured those jointed wooden toys where you push the base and the figure collapses on its strings, then springs back into alignment when released.

Why am I even crying? she wondered as eventually her body calmed. A question of vast curiosity.

It seemed to have something to do with Wasim's daughter, as well as the terrible closeness and the terrible distance of the fitting room. And the ferryman she used to dream about, like an imaginary childhood friend who never arrived. And maybe also something to do with a star she'd once befriended, a star she'd promised—what was it she'd promised? She couldn't remember now. Only the feeling of a fat, round, wordless understanding. A vow without language. And the faint rocking motion of the car as it had ferried her through the night.

How she missed Coco! The little leather book had never turned up, but remained mysteriously lost ever since that day she'd packed it so carefully in her knapsack to take to Rav Harriett's. New hot tears welled up as if from a spring deep inside and coursed rather wonderfully down her cheeks.

Danny would never cry like this, thought Annamae. If only I could be like Danny.

But did she wish it really?

She did not.

What a strange creature, thought Annamae, with benevolence and detachment. She meant herself. The phrase just popped into her mind. If there was a wildlife documentary about her, it was something the narrator might say.

Four Blows

Then came four blows in a row.

The first was that Rav Harriett went away. It was only temporary, but still. She was going to a place called Antwerp for two months to stay with her daughter, who had married some Belgian guy and now was about to have a baby. (Upon hearing this, Danny had turned to Annamae and remarked cheerily, "Ann *twerp*.") Annamae hadn't even known Rav Harriett had a daughter, which was somehow the worst part.

Actually, no. The worst part was that Rav Harriett came for dinner before she left and Annamae had to hear her mother say not once but twice how grateful she was for "all the work you've done with Annamae."

The second time she said it, Rav Harriett was quick to respond, "I'd hardly call it work, Jo," and she shot Annamae a look tinged with knowing, like a wordless phrase from their lexicon built for two. Which helped, but only a little. Because who knew if she said it because she really meant it, or only to spare Annamae's feelings? Their last session had been the one that ended with Annamae picking at a hole in her jeans.

Next their mother announced she was spending the whole weekend of Nobomi's wedding in Maryland.

"Why do you have to go for the whole weekend?" complained Annamae.

"I don't have to. I want to," said her mother.

Annamae and Danny would have to stay at Nana's.

"I can't," said Danny. "That's the tournament."

One phone call later, a new plan was in place: He would spend the weekend at Dante's.

"What about me?" asked Annamae. She had that sensation she got at the beach when she stood at the edge of the water and each time the waves rushed out, a little more of the sand beneath her feet got dragged away.

"You'll go to Nana's."

"By myself?"

"Annamae."

"Can't I go to Maryland with you? I can stay in the hotel while you're at the wedding."

"No."

"Then I'll stay with Felice."

Her mother squinted at her, stroking her invisible mustache. "You want to give her a call?" she finally said.

Felice asked her mother. Her mother agreed. It was all settled, and then the Thursday before the Friday Annamae was to have brought her weekend bag with her to school, Felice was absent.

"They think it's mono," Felice reported over the phone that afternoon. She added importantly, "I'm exhausted."

"Oh," said Annamae. "That's too bad."

"The doctor said I might miss a week or more of school."

"Wow. Well, don't worry about this weekend. We can just stay in and do quiet things. I can read while you nap."

Felice gave a modified, feeble-sounding version of her pealing laughter. "Annamae, you can't come! I'm extremely contagious. And he said I majorly need rest. It affects your spleen and stuff."

Annamae's mother called Nana. "Mom? You're back on duty."

That was the third blow.

The next morning, her necklace went missing.

"Annamae Galinsky!" her mother yelled from the

vestibule at the bottom of the stairs. "We have to go. Now." Her mother was frazzled because her whole timetable had been thrown off by the change in plans. Now instead of heading directly to Baltimore, she had to drive Annamae to Nana's house first. At least it was sort of on the way, but it meant she wasn't going to get there as early as she'd hoped. ("What difference does it make? The wedding's tomorrow," Annamae had said. But it turned out there was something called a rehearsal dinner tonight, and then her mother revealed that she was also planning to meet up with Bev and Ines, friends from the language lab, "to get our nails done," a phrase Annamae had never before heard come out of her mother's mouth.)

"Annamae! What is the problem?"

The question reached her faintly, where she was rummaging through her bedroom two floors up. Like a cobweb or a grave rubbing. Something abstracted from its source.

It was very mysterious. To lose her message-in-a-bottle necklace when she'd been wearing it, when she'd been out and about and the chain might have broken, would have been one thing. But she was absolutely certain she'd taken it off before her bath last night and put it as she always did in the little drawer built into the base of the mirror that sat on her dresser.

She'd already checked the drawer multiple times, as well as her dresser top, her underwear and sock drawers, and the floor below her dresser. Now she used all her might to inch the dresser away from the wall in case it had fallen behind. She found a barrette, a sock, a very large dust bunny, and a single Smarties candy.

Here came her mother up two flights of stairs. Each tread eloquent with impatience.

Annamae shook out the contents of her weekend bag, just in case.

"What's going on?" Her mother stood panting in the doorway. "I thought you were all packed."

"I can't find the necklace Nobomi gave me."

How large, how large that her mother was not dismissive. She remained a moment in the doorway, saying nothing, then began to help Annamae look. They looked everywhere together—in the old toy chest at the foot of the bed, underneath the clothes in the laundry basket, in her bedclothes, and under her mattress.

"I wanted to wear it especially. If I can't be at her wedding. To at least be wearing it on her wedding day."

"I'm sorry," said her mother, "but we do have to leave now."

Annamae went back to her dresser and rummaged again in her underwear drawer.

"Annamae, stop. I need you to listen to me."

"I can't find it! I can't find anything!"

"I'm sorry." Her mother put her arm around her, but it wasn't a real embrace. It was an embrace with a purpose: to steer her toward the door. "Poor Anomenon," her mother added. Annamae could hear the real love her mother poured into the old pet name.

Coldly, Annamae said, "Please don't call me that anymore."

That was the fourth blow. The worse for being self-inflicted.

Nowhere

The moment they walked into Nana's house, the waiting room smell hit Annamae like a perfume ad in a magazine. She turned to her mother, wrinkling her nose.

"How are we?" Nana greeted them in a singsong.

"We're a little out of sorts," Annamae's mother sang back.

"Why," said Annamae furiously, "is everybody using the royal *we*?"

Nana looked from one to the other like they were cards in a game of solitaire and she was calculating the most optimal move.

"I'm sorry, Mom," Annamae's mother said meaningfully.

"Mom!" protested Annamae.

"Don't be sorry, Jo," said Nana. Then added out of the side of her mouth, "And certainly don't *say* sorry."

"Yeah," said Annamae. She accidentally caught Nana's eye and smirked, which made Nana laugh, which gave her mother the impression it was all right for *her* to laugh, too, which it was not; it was adding insult to injury, and Annamae found herself pushing her mother, imploring, "Just *go*, Mom. Just *go*."

Nana walked her mother to the car. Annamae remained in the front hall, looking out of one of the skinny windows that flanked the front door. They were covered with a frosty leaf pattern that chopped the view to bits. "Privacy glass," Nana called it, but if you stood with your face very close, you could see between the leaves. This is what Annamae did;

she stood with her face very close and watched chopped-up bits of her mother and Nana talking in the driveway. Then her mother got in the car and drove away.

"Well," said Nana when she came back in. "We've got a packed agenda."

"What do you mean?"

Nana proceeded to lay it out: Brunch, dry cleaning, post office, library, icebox cake, constitutionals—

"What's that?"

An old-fashioned word for taking a walk. "To improve one's constitution," said Nana, rolling the *r* theatrically.

Annamae studied Nana's eyes. They weren't doing that darty thing. "I'm glad your ataxia's better."

"You and me both."

And tomorrow if the weather held, they could ride the ferry.

"What ferry?"

The ferry landing in Nana's town. Annamae had forgotten about that, how when she and Danny were little, they used to go watch the ferries dock and depart.

"Where will we ride it to?" asked Annamae.

"Nowhere!" As if that's what made it a treat.

Bugle

After brunch (French toast), they went to the dry cleaner's, which smelled of even more chemicals than Nana's furniture polish. Annamae said, "I'll wait outside," and stood on the sidewalk while Nana dropped off her cleaning.

The dry cleaner's display window held an enormous white box shaped like a book. The lid was hinged open so you could see inside, where, instead of words, an oval window let you peek at the torso of a satiny white gown fitted on some sort of mold to make it look like it was on an actual woman's body. A woman's body that had been sawed in half by a magician. On what was meant to look like the inside front cover, in cursive so ornate you could barely read it, it said *Make Your Day Last Forever.*

It was like one of those crazy books from Art Explorers. Not the ones they'd made themselves, but the sculpturey ones Leslie had shown them on her phone. The glory of it: to think that the secret world of a book could be unlocked with a knife. The invertedness of it: to think that by cutting away, you could create more. That something lay beyond the flatness of paper, the flatness of words. Hadn't one of the books opened to reveal ocean waves and a many-masted sailing ship rising up from the pages? Hadn't another been carved in such a way that you could gaze upon a spiral staircase that seemed to wind down, down into a whole other world below the surface?

What a disappointment it had been when she'd tried it herself with the paring knife and gotten yelled at.

When Nana came out, the bell on the door tinkling behind her, she saw Annamae gazing at the display and mistook the reason for her interest. "I remember I loved to look at wedding gowns, too," she said. "Starting around your age."

"I don't really care for them."

Nana made a flabbergasted face. "You are a preternaturally serious girl."

Annamae was not offended. The opposite.

"Well, in any case," Nana went on, walking not toward the car but toward a little plaza where the sidewalk widened and had been appointed with trees and benches, "I remember staring with great longing into the window of the bridal shop on my way home from school."

"Longing for what?"

They sat on a bench. The branches were frilly with young leaves.

"That's interesting, Annamae. You're right. I guess it wasn't really longing for a *dress*. Although I did think they were beautiful. And it wasn't—it wasn't really a longing to get married. Certainly not at that age. You're eleven?"

"Twelve."

"Still." Nana stuck out her legs and crossed them at the ankles. Pigeons pecked at a piece of bread with mustard on it. "Now that you get me thinking, I suppose it was probably more of a generalized longing. The bridal gowns were some kind of—oh, I don't know, reveille—"

"What's that?"

"You know." Nana *doot doot doodle-ooted* the melody. At least three passersby looked over and smiled. "That bugle song they play in the army to wake up soldiers. Maybe the bridal gowns weren't really what I desired. They were just the bugle."

"What do you mean?"

"A kind of call, waking me up to a longing I'd never experienced before."

"But what was the longing for?"

"Well . . . I suppose it was to see what the future held in store."

"You said you didn't believe in fortune-telling."

Nana laughed. "I hope I'm never cross-examined by you in a court of law. Okay, maybe it wasn't a longing to know. Maybe it was just a longing to be on my way."

"On your way to what?"

"Whatever I was headed toward."

Thumb Trick

After supper (meat loaf and icebox cake), it was both warm enough and light enough to take books out on the porch. Nana had two big chairs ("What are those called again?" "Adirondack chairs") and two big bushes, one on either side of the steps, heavy with clusters of teeny purple flowers ("What are those called again?" "Lilacs"). Her neighborhood was peaceful and boring. Occasionally, someone walked by with a dog; that was it.

"How's your book?" asked Nana after a while.

"Good. I've read it before. How's yours?"

"In progress." Nana held it up to show Annamae the cover. FIVE YEAR DIARY was stamped in gold.

"I didn't know you kept a diary."

"I've been keeping one for decades. Though it's not really a diary."

"It says *diary*."

"But look." Nana showed her how the book was laid out. This was the third year of five, so the two sections above today's entry were already filled in with Nana's distinctively slanty script, telling what she'd done on this exact day last year and the year before. The two sections below were empty, waiting for next year and the one after that. "You can see there's just enough room to record a few lines per day. More of a captain's log than a diary."

"What do you mean, a captain's log?"

"Basic, minimal facts. I guess a real captain's log would record things like latitude and longitude, weather.

Provisions, supplies. Any passengers you happen to take on or let off."

"Did you put me in for today?"

Nana read aloud: "Jo brought Annamae for weekend while she attends wedding in Balt. Took comforter and wool coat to cleaner's. P.O., library. Meat loaf, peas, Ellen's pilaf. A. made icebox cake. Weather mild. Lilacs at peak."

"Who's Ellen?"

"The friend who gave me the recipe for the pilaf."

"That was good."

"Did you like it?"

Annamae nodded. Nana's neighborhood was boring, but it had more sky. The sky was huge and lavender. Already you could see the moon.

"Do you still keep a diary?" asked Nana.

"I never did that."

"No? I thought there was one you used to carry around with you wherever you went."

"That's not a diary. That's my notebook. Coco. I lost it."

"Would you like to borrow some writing paper?"

Annamae nodded.

Together, they went inside the house. It smelled more like life now, like meat loaf and lilacs and dusk. Nana went to the piece of furniture she called a "secretary" and opened the hinged top. There were cubbies inside with cream-colored stationery and envelopes and stamps. Nana took out a few sheets of stationery. Then she set them down and took out a little notebook instead. "Do you think you'd like to have this? The first couple of pages have notes I took for a class, but you could just tear them out."

"What class?"

"Oh." Nana looked embarrassed. "An adult education class. On the cosmos. I think most of the students must have had some background in physics. I couldn't keep up. Here's a straightedge, let's just tea—"

"No." Annamae laid a hand on Nana's arm. "Leave them."

They looked over what Nana had written:

There was a diagram showing spheres and orbits with dotted lines between them and the labels: EARTH, SUN, STARS, DISTANCE.

"What's that about?" asked Annamae.

Nana scrunched up her nose. "I think we were learning how to measure the distance to the stars."

On the next page was a feast of unknown words and terms:

STANDARD CANDLES
CEPHEID VARIABLES
HUBBLE LAW
PARSEC
SEXTANT
CELESTIAL NAVIGATION
STELLAR PARALLAX
SECULAR PARALLAX
THUMB TRICK

"What's *parallax?*" Annamae asked.

"Oh honey. I want to say something to do with sailors? A way of measuring distance maybe? Between yourself and an unknown object—or no, between the horizon and a star?"

"What's *thumb trick?*" Annamae asked.

"That one I actually think I remember." Nana closed her eyes a moment, then opened them again. "Yes. Okay, pick an object on the other side of the room."

They both turned to face the far wall.

"Got one?"

"The clock."

"Okay. Wait, can you wink?"

"Sort of."

"Okay. Hold out your thumb and wink one eye shut so the clock's completely covered."

"Okay."

"Now, keeping your thumb exactly where it is, open that eye and shut the other."

"Oh!"

"Did it jump?"

It had. The clock had jumped several feet to the left.

"You know what that proves?" said Annamae with sudden inspiration. She might be a little bit of a genius herself.

"What does it prove?"

"That it's impossible ever to see eye to eye—even with yourself."

Captain's Log

That night, propped against the pink headboard of her mother's childhood bed, Annamae took Nana's old notebook off the bedside table. It was bound in flowered corduroy instead of leather, and its pages were lined instead of blank. Unlike Coco, it had not been hers from the beginning. Like the dollhouse, it bore marks made by an earlier owner, someone deeply familiar to her and unknowable all the same.

She opened it to the first blank page and wrote:

> *Mom went to Balt. for Nobomi's wedding. D. at Dante's. N. gave me this journal. Made rice pilaf, meat loaf (N.) & icebox cake (me). I'm ~~actually~~ having a nice time with N.*

Underneath, she made a diagram showing someone blowing into a horn beneath a constellation in the shape of a question mark. She drew some dotted lines and added the labels: ME, STARS, UNKNOWN OBJECT, DISTANCE.

Correspondence

The weather did not hold. Saturday morning was damp and gray.

"We could still go," suggested Annamae, meaning the ferry.

"I'm afraid we won't enjoy it," said Nana, "if we're chilly and there's nothing to see."

"What are we going to do instead?"

Nana dunked her tea bag up and down in her mug. "That is the question."

"It's not a question of agenda; it's a question *about* the agenda!" crowed Annamae.

Nana didn't get it.

After breakfast (cereal and blueberries), Nana played solitaire on the computer while Annamae read. "Stall tactics," Nana called it, in case the weather lifted. But by midmorning, rain was coming down. By noon, Annamae had finished her book. "We should have had you check out a stack," Nana said. After lunch (grilled cheese and oranges), Nana played more computer solitaire and Annamae used some of her cream-colored stationery to write letters.

"Dear Felice," she wrote, and told about almost riding the ferry but then not. "Dear Nobomi," she wrote, and told about losing the message-in-a-bottle necklace. "Dear Mr. T.," she wrote, and told about Nana's question *about* an agenda. "Dear Leslie," she wrote, and told about the wedding dress inside the book-shaped box. "Dear Rav Harriett," she wrote, and told about reveille and longing. "Dear

Wasim's Daughter," she wrote, and told about tossing apple peels over your shoulder. "Dear Freddie Festano," she wrote, and told about measuring the distance between herself and a star. "Dear Star," she wrote, and told about forgetting what she had vowed. "Dear Lighting Shop," she wrote, and told about the bakery and the dog salon and the hair salon and the hardware store that used to be in its place. "Dear Sixty Panes of Glass," she wrote, and told about the beehive windows of the office building across the street. "Dear Ferryman," she wrote, and told about posting him messages through the folds of the accordion radiator. "Dear ———," she wrote, because there was someone else she meant to address—was meant to address—whose name she did not know. What came out was a kind of poem. She didn't think it up; all she did was write it down:

Many times I have seen you
But you have not seen me

Wandering
You call my name

I hold out my hand
You don't see

Still I have been singing
I am singing to you now

In Motion

"Oh," said Nana. "I had no idea you were going to use so much stationery. Is that all one letter? It's *how* many? Do you need envelopes for all twelve?"

Felice's was the only address she knew. "Just one, please."

"All right, help yourself. You'll find a stamp in the drawer."

Annamae prepared Felice's letter for mailing.

"You can leave it in the mailbox on the porch," said Nana.

"But that's where you get your mail delivered."

"The mail carrier will take it when she brings mine."

Annamae stepped outside. The lilacs were dripping, but the rain had let up. She felt like a dog that's been swimming. The way they look at the beach, their wild energy when they come onto the shore, the way they shake the water off their fur and go bounding in circles, happy just to be in motion. Writing all those letters, she'd been immersed. Now that she was done, some kind of elation needed to be spent.

"Nana." She stepped back into the house. "I'm going to take a walk."

"Where? In the rain?"

"It stopped. I'll walk to the mailbox."

Nana came into the front hall. "Do you want me to go with you?"

"No, that's okay. I just feel like walking."

"The mailbox is right on the corner."

"Okay. I'll probably go for a longer walk than that, though."

They went onto the porch together.

"It's still coming down," said Nana.

"Just mist."

"Well, take my raincoat."

"I don't think I need it," said Annamae.

"Take it anyway, honey. It might start up again. Where will you walk?"

"I don't know. Around. Don't worry, Nana. I'm used to getting around the city by myself."

"I suppose that's true. Are you sure you don't want company?"

"No, I'm good."

The rain had knocked early-spring petals and catkins off the trees, strewing the ground with color. The puddles were festooned with pollen and oil. Annamae had never been out walking by herself in the country. A million times in the city, but to walk alone in the country was something new. Of course this wasn't really the country, but it was unfamiliar. To walk somewhere unfamiliar, alone, was new.

She reached the corner mailbox and put the one envelope addressed to Felice in the slot. She remembered how she and Danny used to fight over who got to open the mailbox door. She wondered how his basketball tournament was going. She remembered Nobomi was getting married today, maybe right this very second. It all seemed far away. This world, this immediate, unfamiliar, dripping green and pink and iridescent world, was at hand.

Where to now?

She'd rolled up the other letters—or poems or riddles or songs or prayers, whatever they were—and stuck them in her pocket, the pocket of Nana's raincoat, as she was leaving. She took them out now, as if consulting a map, as if they might tell her where to head. They did, sort of. It came to her that she should post them. An idea both funny and serious.

Replacing the sheaf of papers in Nana's pocket, her fingers grazed something at the bottom. She pulled it out. Actually, three things: a tissue, a mint, a penny. The tissue she stuffed back in the pocket. The mint she popped into her mouth. With the penny, she knew exactly what to do.

Two Beginnings and No End

Quickly then (because you know what comes next)—

She played the penny game. Heads right, tails left. The penny took her past houses, wove her into town. Sent her by the dry cleaner's and angled her right through yesterday's little plaza. Hello, pigeons. Hello, bread with mustard.

It took her down a road more like an alley, deserted except for a single cat perched on top of a dumpster. It turned its head to watch her, lashing its tail.

She thought she ought to feel nervous, or at least very alone, but she didn't feel alone at all. She felt unaccountably, emphatically accompanied.

When she came out of the alley, ready to flip the penny and receive her next instruction, she almost

to retract it, she lost her balance and began to fall.

Now in such rapid succession all four things seemed to happen at once: I flung out a hand to catch her; the necklace broke; I caught her by the scruff; the bottle slipped beneath the skin of the sea.

Once again I plunged my arm into the water. Too late. It sunk down, down, out of reach, out of sight.

What kind of stoppered bottle sinks?

I filled with wonder. I filled with recognition. My search had begun.

to continue with "Fro."

laughed: across the street, beyond a parking lot, the ferry terminal!

Flooded with urgent joy, she broke into a run. But upon crossing the length of the parking lot, she met another intersection: a bicycle path. Dutifully, she consulted the penny: tails. Tails sent her away from the ferry terminal, toward a little jetty instead.

Curious, up for the adventure, she picked her way out along the rocks, navigating carefully all the way to the end, where she sat. It was barely misting anymore. Just the faintest moisture. As if the rain were kissing her. The river was dark and wide and windswept. Its waves wore triangular white caps.

What a thing! To be twelve and alone and perched on a rock jutting into the river.

No one, not a soul, knew where she was, and yet she was not lost.

Taking the sheaf of papers from the pocket of Nana's raincoat, she posted

a long paw, just as she had done at the ferry landing.

I picked my way across the jagged, slippery rocks as quickly as I dared, then lay on my stomach beside her and looked, expecting to find her provoked again by her own reflection. But no.

Something else this time: a coppery fish deep in the murk, growing brighter as it swam toward the surface. It rose, revolving, flipping over and over. Such a strange-looking fish, flat and round as a disc. Company swiped and missed.

"Hang on, I'll get it." I shoved up my sleeve and dragged my hand through the water, closed my fist on something, and brought it up, dripping. When I opened my hand, I was looking at a metal coin.

What kind of metal coin floats?

Company swiped again, this time at me, or the tiny corked bottle dangling from my neck. One of her claws snagged in the chain. Trying them. One by one she fed them to the current, ending with the message addressed: “Dear ———.”

The waves carried the pieces of cream-colored stationery downriver toward what she knew was the sea. She watched until she could no longer see them, then studied the movement of the water until it felt like she was in motion, too.

Which of course, being in the world, she was.

She sneezed. And fished for the tissue in Nana's pocket. When it came out, the penny came, too. Flipped through the air and plopped into the water. She thrust in her arm to grasp it. Too late.

She stared at the place where it had sunk, as if it might rise again. Like a raisin in seltzer. Ninny, she thought.

But there was something. A glint of silver. Reaching in, she grasped a chain on which was threaded a little glass bottle. With—yes—a tiny paper scroll inside.

She stared at it on her dripping palm. No one, no

Many times I have seen you
But you have not seen me

“Shall we go to sea, Company? What would you think of that?”

The song's plainness helped it carry clearly on the wind.

Wandering
You call my name

I hold out my hand
You don't see

“We're going to sea,” I declared. Then: “Where to now?” for the kitten was venturing farther along the jetty, sniffing at barnacles, inspecting long tendrils of seaweed undulating like shadows in the shallows.

The sailors kept singing. A trick of the wind made the music seem to be coming from inside my own head.

Still I have been singing
I am singing to you now

The kitten reached the very end of the jetty, where she stood like a bowsprit against the breeze. Then something in the water must have caught her eye. She crouched low and extended one could call this science. Nor could they call the penny game science. Nor posting letters on waves. Or the thing Leslie had taught them:

Visualize something rising up through water.

Visualize something floating down into your hands.

A beautiful hunger unfurled inside of her. Closing her eyes, she turned her palms to the sky.

to continue with "To"

Two Beginnings and No End

The harbor: seabirds and ships. Activity, movement. Immense white sails. Everywhere I looked something was happening. Flooded by urgent joy, I broke into a run.

On the docks crates were being lifted with ropes. "Get out of the way!" someone yelled. In the next slip we saw fish being unloaded. "Watch yourself—it's slick," someone hollered, just in time for us to skirt a greasy puddle of guts.

We left the docks and headed for the strand where we wouldn't be in the way, then wandered out along some rocks that stuck into the bay.

From a ship where they were hoisting the sails we heard sailors singing. I recognized the song.